HmF

PRAISE

Selected as one of the ~~~
Roberts' DARK WITCH and Julia ~~~
KISSES. USA Today Contributor, Becky Lower, Happ~~ ~r
After

"Ava's story is witty and charming." Barbara Freethy #1 NYT
bestselling author

FRENCH ROAST
"An entertaining ride...{and) a full-bodied romance." Readers'
Favorite

THE GRAND OPENING
"Ava Miles is fast becoming one of my favorite light
contemporary romance writers." Tome Tender

THE HOLIDAY SERENADE
"This story is all romance, steam, and humor with a touch of
the holiday spirit..." The Book Nympho

THE TOWN SQUARE
"Ms. Miles' words melted into each page until the world
receded around me..." Tome Tender

COUNTRY HEAVEN
"If ever there was a contemporary romance that rated a 10 on
a scale of 1 to 5 for me, this one is it!" The Romance Reviews

THE PARK OF SUNSET DREAMS
"Ava has done it again. I love the whole community of Dare
Valley..." Travel Through The Pages Blog

THE CHOCOLATE GARDEN
"On par with Nicholas Sparks' love stories." Jennifer's Corner
Blog

USA TODAY BESTSELLING AUTHOR

AVA MILES

Daring
Brides

THE
DARE VALLEY SERIES

This is a work of fiction. All of the characters, organizations, and events portrayed in this novel are either the products of the author's imagination or are used fictionally.

ISBN-13: 978-1-940565-31-6
www.avamiles.com
Ava Miles

To my sister, Michelle Khamis, wedding planner extraordinaire—here's to following our dreams, being successful entrepreneurs, living a joyful and abundant life, and supporting each other throughout the journey.

And to my divine entourage, who helps me see the joy and beauty of marriage all over again.

Acknowledgements

Team Ava is the absolute best: Sienna, Angela, Louisa, Em, Hilary, Leigh, Beth, and my Angels. They support me in all the ways I need with absolute efficiency and joy. Yeah!

As I said, my sister, Michelle Khamis, helped me envision all these weddings so they'd be top notch and true-to-life. She went from being my inspiration in NORA ROBERTS LAND to starting her own business and being named Best Wedding Planner of the Year. Thanks for the vision boards for each wedding and for adding to the Daring Brides Pinterest board to give a canvas to this story.

T.F. My favorite mental image right now is of you standing at the end of the aisle.

And finally, to all my readers, who wanted to see the weddings of our favorite Dare Valley couples—so far. This one is for you.

The Grand Mountain Hotel

Emmits Merriam University
The Hale School of Journalism

Washington
Elementary School

The Western
Independent

Barber Shop

OAK ST.

Fire Station

Hairy's Pub

Don't Soy
With Me

Smith's Hardware

PONDEROSA ST.

Brasserie Dare

Kemstead's
Bakery

Don't Wedge
Me In

ASPEN ST.

Community Center

The Chop House

Justice Center

MAPLE ST.

MAIN ST.

DARE VALLEY, CO
Population 20,909   Elevation 9400 ft.

Thorn's Peak

MEREDITH & TANNER

Meredith Hale's first wedding had been packed with so much pomp and circumstance that it wouldn't have seemed out of place if the Ringling Bros. and Barnum & Bailey had joined the melee with elephants. Of course, her then-groom was the one who'd insisted on the spectacle. She should have seen Rick-the-Dick's wedding egomania for what it was—another indication they weren't truly suited, that they wouldn't truly last. Five hundred people had packed into St. Patrick's Cathedral in New York City. Their reception had been sumptuously hosted by The Plaza on Fifth Avenue. She hadn't known over half of the guests.

When she and her own Nora-Roberts-hero fiancé, Tanner McBride, had sat down to plan their wedding— her second and his first—they had been in complete accord. A small gathering. Only family and friends. Not super dressy, but with a great band and awesome food.

As she stood in front of the full-length mirror in the church's bridal area, watching her mother fluff her veil, she realized how different she felt from the last time she'd worn a wedding dress. Before, her chest had been tight with pressure. Today, she felt all gooey inside. The kind of gooey that could only come from true love.

She'd returned to Dare Valley to prove that heroes

like the men in Nora Roberts novels really existed—despite what her ex-husband, Rick-the-Dick, had said to the contrary.

She'd more than proved it. She'd found one for herself. And all because of that quality her grandpa called daring.

"Mom," she said softly. "I think my veil is fluffy enough, don't you?" It was lace trim, matching her dress, and trailed to mid-back. There was no way she was covering her face.

"Any more fluff, and it would be cotton candy," her sister said from her perch on the small sofa, smoothing a hand over her red silk dress.

Jill was her only bridesmaid today, whereas last time she'd had seven. *Seven.* What had she been thinking?

"I'll fluff it all I want, thank you very much," their mom, Linda, responded with an exaggerated eye roll.

"You're a lot more chill this time," Jill commented, unscrewing the perfume bottle Meredith had brought and taking a sniff. "Of course, that's mostly because you're marrying the best man in the world this time and not an asshole."

Leave it to Jill to put it out there. "I couldn't agree more. What's the time?"

Jill dabbed some perfume behind her ears and then reached into her bold purple purse for her phone. "We have a bit of time yet. How about a mimosa? I smuggled the fixings into one of my bags. I brought enough to fuel an army, and there are even special wedding straws so we won't mess up our lipstick."

She held up a bunch of straws decorated with red hearts on a white background. Where did her sister find such things?

"The church doesn't allow alcohol inside, Jill," their mother said, looking toward the door as if they were doing something naughty. "But I won't tell if you won't."

Jill stuck her free hand out, and they shook on it. "Deal."

Wonderful. The party was going to start early. "Okay, why not? I am duly made up and everything."

"Tanner looks pretty hot," Jill said, waggling her reddish-brown eyebrows. "I peeked earlier when I went to confer with the vocalist. She and the piano player seem cool."

"They are," she told her sister.

Her cousin, Caroline Hale, had helped her find the vocalist in Denver. "Where are Natalie, Caroline, and Moira, by the way?" Even though it was a small wedding, she was still trying to keep track of everyone and be a wonderful hostess. Her cousins had arrived early this morning with her aunt and uncle from Denver, but had disappeared after Meredith changed into her wedding dress. Tanner's sister, Peggy McBride, was off with the guys since such a profusion of dresses and makeup and tears would give her hives.

"Grandpa Hale is holding court in the vestibule," Jill told her. "He was showing Danny his disappearing-coin-behind-the-ear trick. Do you remember when he taught that one to Andy and Matt when we were kids?"

Her uncle and aunt had five kids, two boys and three girls. They were about the same age as Meredith and Jill, but they'd moved to Denver fifteen years ago so her uncle could take a more prestigious position at one of the hospitals there.

"Matt pretended to swallow the coin," she said, touching up her pink nude lipstick at the corners. "Aunt April was halfway to the emergency room by the time Matt confessed it was a gag."

"April was mad enough to see red that day," her mom said, shaking her head. "I never envied her for raising boys. Now, it seems like your grandfather is passing on his tricks to the next generation. We'll all need to watch out."

"Danny is only four, mom," Meredith said. "And it's good to see him learning something as silly as one of grandpa's magic tricks after losing his mom."

Andy's wife had passed away from breast cancer just last year, at the tender age of thirty, and the whole family had been devastated. This was the first family event since Kim's funeral, and she wanted everyone to have a good time.

"Andy still looks gaunt to me," her mom said, clucking her tongue. "And Natalie worries me too. She's looked so unhappy ever since things fell apart with Blake."

Jill heaved a deep sigh. "I know. It's still a bit of a shock. I loved that guy."

"We all did," Meredith said, thinking about her own divorce. Blake Cunningham, the quarterback for the Denver Raiders, was nothing like Rick-the-Dick. Sure, they were both powerful and famous men in their own right, but Blake had a huge heart and Richard Sommerville... Well, he'd captured her by being at once mesmerizing and aggressive. Thank God her taste in men had changed.

"All right," her mom said. "Enough of the past. Today's about new beginnings. Your father and I couldn't be happier for you, honey. Tanner *is* the best man in the world, just like your sister said. For you."

"I know it," she said, feeling that warm glow in her heart expand at the mere thought of him.

The door to the room opened, and her three cousins and Aunt April bustled inside.

"We told the men it was girls only," Moira said with a small smile. "Your grandpa huffed and puffed like the big bad wolf, but he looked mostly relieved."

"He's a big faker," Caroline said, setting down her clutch purse on the sofa's arm. "Earlier, he kept teasing us about dolling up our faces with sparkles and saying women in his day never bothered with such nonsense."

"What a load of crap. Grandma Harriet wore makeup all her life," Meredith said with a slight pinch to her heart. "I wish she were here today."

"She is, honey," her mom said, taking her hands. "Now, let's do one last inspection now that the rest of the girls are here and then have those mimosas Jill is making for everyone."

Moira gave a cat-call whistle, and a few of them joined in with squeals, which made Meredith laugh.

She stepped in front of the full-length mirror again. Her gown was made of lace and pearl beads, which were stitched into a coronet pattern at her waist. The dress had the most delicate straps imaginable, and the bodice was an understated sweetheart. It fell to her feet, snugly fitting her body, and didn't have a train. She'd decided to let her veil convey that touch of whimsy.

"You look beautiful, Mermaid," Jill told her as she poured orange juice and champagne into pink *Here Comes the Bride* plastic cups.

"You really do," Aunt April said, to which her daughters all nodded in agreement.

If the tight line of her mouth was any indication, Natalie was more than a little uncomfortable, and Meredith wondered whether she was thinking about her own wedding to Blake. It had been a casual beach wedding in Santa Cruz.

"Everything looks under control in here," Natalie said, walking over and kissing her cheek. "I'm going to find the boys and make sure we get a good seat. If you need anything, just remember, I have the wedding emergency kit."

"Jill's acting like a drama queen," she told her cousin. "Unless things go horribly wrong, we shouldn't need anything that's in there. What'd she stock it with, anyway? Stain-removal wipes, safety pins, and—"

"Static cling spray," her sister finished with a glower. "You never know what could happen. I saw a wedding episode once where the bride's veil got so much static cling her hair ended up looking like the bride of Frankenstein's."

Everyone chuckled as Natalie gave a wave and headed out. Meredith's heart went out to her. She knew all too well how much divorce could hurt, and it was even worse for Nat because of how devoted she and Blake had been to each other before Kim died.

"She's thinking about Blake," Moira said, echoing her thoughts.

"She's just not over him," Caroline murmured. "I wish we could help her."

Aunt April wrapped her arms around them. "I know you do. We all do. But your sister's stubborn, and she's going to have to decide to do something about it on her own. And that's enough talk about that."

"Jill, why don't you pass those mimosas around?" Meredith asked, sensing everyone wanted to focus on happier things. "You're being remiss in your bartending duties."

Her sister wiggled her hips. "I'll show you some action."

When everyone had a mimosa in hand, Jill raised her glass. "To finding your Nora Roberts hero."

Everyone gave a heartfelt sigh.

And as she drank her fruity concoction, Meredith took a moment to bask in gratitude and happiness once again for the quest that had brought her to Dare Valley, and subsequently to Tanner McBride.

***

Tanner McBride had never imagined he would get married. When he was covering war zones and hopping across the globe from Burma to the Democratic Republic of Congo as a war correspondent, the possibility of meeting some girl and settling down had seemed impossibly distant.

Then again, he'd never imagined coming to Dare Valley, and to be fair, he hadn't come willingly at first. He was man enough to admit there was something bigger than him guiding his steps at times—call it fate or destiny—and he was sure glad it had brought him here, to Meredith.

He and his party were hanging out in a room usually reserved for church meetings and Bible studies. It was presided over by a stained glass window depicting a rose garden and a lone sheep, the meaning of which he couldn't divine.

"I can't wait to sneak away and roam through the Hale School of Journalism during the reception," Asher Harrington, his best man, said in his perfect upper-class British broadcast journalist accent.

Tanner had been delighted his buddy could make it. They'd met years ago in war-torn Beirut at the famous Commodore Hotel over a game of poker, and their paths had crossed several times more in other places riddled with bullets and blood. Women swooned over Asher wherever he went. Fortunately, Tanner's sister, who had opted to spend the pre-wedding hour with him rather than with Meredith and the other Hale women, was immune to the journalist's accent and looks. Peggy McBride was the new deputy sheriff in town, and she looked as tough on the outside in her black pantsuit as the perfectly coiffed Asher was on the inside. While Tanner's debonair friend never had a hair out of place, his looks were deceiving. Tanner had seen him stand down a tank in Afghanistan once.

"I'm sure Arthur Hale will give you a tour if you ask him," Peggy said from one of the brown-clad chairs in the room.

"Can I come too?" her son, Keith, asked, bouncing on the chair next to hers.

Tanner swept the seven-year-old into his arms for a

quick hug. "You bet." If he hadn't been so eager to spend every moment of the reception with his bride, he would have offered to give them a tour himself.

Because he was an adjunct professor at the Hale School of Journalism, he'd struck upon the idea of holding their wedding reception there. Didn't they host banquets for award-winning journalists and other events? Why not a wedding reception?

Meredith, being a journalist herself, had loved the idea, and her cousin, Natalie, had agreed to cater the event. Arthur had been preening like a peacock from the moment they'd announced their engagement, and the news that the event would be held in a school of journalism had only amplified his excitement. He was imagining all of the baby journalists Tanner and Meredith would create together, ensuring his famous newspaper, *The Western Independent*, stayed in the Hale family for generations to come.

His phone rang, and he checked the display. His brother. David hadn't been able to make it to the wedding due to his wife's advancing pregnancy, and it was probably for the best. They weren't on good terms right now, which he hoped would change.

"Hi, David," he said when he answered.

"I know you're busy since it's getting close to the ceremony, but I was thinking about you and wanted to wish you congratulations on your big day."

"Thanks," he replied. "I'm just hanging out with Peggy and Keith and my best man."

"Tell them all hello," David said. Then, abruptly, "Well, I'll let you go."

"It was nice of you to call, David."

"Bye, Tanner," he simply said and clicked off.

Peggy didn't say anything, but she didn't need to. The frown on her face said it all.

"Peggy, weren't you going to show me your version of the chokehold?" Asher asked. The note of forced cheer in his voice told Tanner he hadn't missed the tension in the room.

Leave it to his best man and his sister to bond over chokehold techniques.

"I still can't believe someone as pretty as you even knows what one is," Peggy said with some sauce in her tone.

"Many have been fooled by this face," Asher said, holding up a hand to the profile Tanner had seen dozens of women drool over.

"All right," Peggy said, standing up and planting her feet. "Show me what you've got."

As Peggy and Asher circled each other, Tanner extended his hand to Keith. "How about you and I go find Arthur?"

The boy simply nodded. "I like our new family." Hearing that was like feeling warm sunshine pour into his heart.

"Me too," he replied and escorted his nephew out of the room before things got too crazy. Peggy was already wrapping her arm around Asher's neck.

Arthur was being his endearing, curmudgeonly self when Tanner and Keith found him in the vestibule with the rest of the males in the Hale family and their single female representative, Natalie. Tanner had met Meredith's Denver cousins already, and they all seemed to be cut from the same cloth as their Dare Valley counterparts.

"Well, well, well," Arthur drolled. "If it isn't the groom. Although it's hard to recognize you as such since you're not wearing a tuxedo."

"I hate monkey suits," Tanner told him with a shrug.

Thank God, Meredith had understood how much he hated formal attire. She'd been okay with his choice of a cream tan suit with an open-collar white shirt. No tie. It was more of a beach look, Jill had told him, but he'd added a splash of panache with the red silk handkerchief in deference to Meredith's choice of red amaryllis flowers for her bouquet.

"Can I have a red hot?" Keith asked the elderly man, who dutifully dug one out of his pant's pocket.

"Do you want one?" Arthur asked, turning to him.

"Better not. It might give me a red tongue, and that would be awkward for when I say, 'I do.'" He stuck his tongue out playfully to Keith, who laughed like he'd just said the silliest thing ever.

"I want a red tongue," Keith said, sticking out his tongue and pointing to it before he popped a candy into his mouth.

"Me too," Danny mimicked.

So far, the two boys had bonded like crazy. Tanner threw Andy a look as if to say, "Kids." The Hale brothers simply laughed and held out their hands as Arthur passed around more red hots. The man was like his own candy machine. Natalie deferred, agreeing with Tanner about the whole red-tongue thing.

"Are you nervous, Tanner?" Alan Hale, his future father-in-law, asked as he accepted a red hot.

Tanner had faced down the Taliban. How could he be nervous about marrying the woman of his dreams in the safe little town of Dare Valley, surrounded by family and friends? "Nope. Not a bit."

"It's getting to be about time," Alan said, tapping his watch face.

"I'll just go and grab my sister and my best man," Tanner said. "That is, if they're both still alive."

Alan blinked rapidly, but Arthur barked out a laugh.

"Not too many men would come out alive after being penned up with your sister," the older man said. "That's why she'll make a great deputy sheriff for our town. What are they doing in there, anyway?"

The Denver cousins, not to mention Meredith's father, looked at Arthur like he'd just asked an inappropriate question, but the older man knew Peggy well enough to know there wasn't any hanky panky going on in the waiting room. "They're trading chokehold techniques."

The other men's eyes widened in shock, but the journalistic legend nodded sagely. "Sounds like a smart swap. You never know when you might need to use a chokehold on someone."

"Dad!" Alan said aghast.

"You never worked international," Arthur said. "It's another world."

After wrangling Asher and his sister, Tanner returned to the vestibule with the two in tow.

"I know you just got back here, but you'd better head to the waiting room with Asher," Alan said, making sure his tie was straight. "The guests are starting to arrive."

Tanner didn't see the harm in staying where he was, but he clapped Asher on the back and off they went. When it came time for the ceremony to begin, he and Asher strolled out and took their places at the altar. All of the guests smiled at him, but his eyes were glued to the front of the church, waiting for that first glimpse of his bride. Covered in a long white runner, the aisle was flanked by candles and red roses, amaryllis, and red hypericum, the latter of which he would never have identified if Meredith hadn't asked him to make a follow-up call to the florist one night.

Bach's "Jesu, Joy of Man's Desiring" swelled, and so did his heart. He smiled as Danny came down the aisle holding an engraved sign that said *Here Comes the Bride*. They'd had to send the first sign back because it had arrived saying *Here Comes the Bird*. Someone needed to use spell check.

Next came Keith, their ring bearer, who beamed with happiness as he made his way up the aisle and came to a stop near the altar.

Looking lovely in a red satin bridesmaid's dress, Jill strutted down the aisle with that sassy smile of hers.

Asher met her halfway, and she curled her fingers around his arm and gave her grandpa a wink as she passed him. Tanner simply shook his head at his soon-to-be sister-in-law, whom he loved not only for all the energy she had poured into matchmaking for him and Meredith, but also for her wicked sense of humor. She blew him a kiss and took her place on the other side of the altar.

Then the music changed to "Ode to Joy," which Meredith had chosen for its name, and everyone in the church stood.

His throat backed up when he saw her. Her red hair was swept up into some kind of elegant coif with soft curls framing her face. A short white veil was tucked into her hair and danced along her mid-back as she walked down the aisle, her blue eyes sparkling. When her dad kissed her cheek and stepped back, she locked gazes with Tanner and didn't glance away. It felt like nothing could pull them apart.

As he took her hand, he knew nothing ever would.

***

Meredith knew everyone oohed and aahed over the bride at weddings, but when she saw Tanner, she decided those people were missing the boat. He was the most handsome groom imaginable. She was so glad he hadn't worn a tux out of convention because his cream tan suit was so much more him. His rugged face softened when their hands met, and his brown eyes shone like the North Star on a recent December night.

"You take my breath away," he whispered to her.

"I was just thinking the same thing."

He flashed her that devilish smile, the same one that had made her heart go pa-rum-pum-pum that first night at Hairy's Irish Pub. It played the same beat now.

They took their places in front of the minister she'd

known all her life, and the ceremony began. Everything else faded away. As she stared into her love's eyes, she heard the minister talk about how they'd met and then her cousins, Caroline and Matt, read the two passages they'd selected. His was "Every Day" by David Levithan while hers was by "Looking For Your Face" by Rumi.

She mouthed the first line to the Rumi poem as it was read.

From the beginning of my life I have been looking for your face, but today I have seen it.

He raised her hand to his mouth and kissed it with such exquisite tenderness she felt tears form in her eyes.

"I love you," he mouthed back, and a single tear cruised down her cheek.

When it came time to say their vows, she took a deep breath. They'd decided to write their own—they were journalists, after all—but mostly, she'd wanted this ceremony to be so different from her first that it was unrecognizable.

"Meredith," Tanner began, holding her hand firmly in his own, "when I came to Dare Valley after traveling the world, I was an empty shell. Burned out. Hollow. I didn't believe there was any good in the world. I certainly didn't believe in romantic love."

She felt a smile touch the corners of her mouth as more tears filled her eyes.

"And then I found you. I know you were looking for someone else, some hero from a Nora Roberts novel. Lucky for me, you think I'm that guy. I don't know about that, but I do know this. I'm the one who loves you every which way, who wants to curl up on the couch with you on these endless winter nights, who wants to explore and enjoy your mind as we work together at the family newspaper your grandfather built. I promise to always be faithful. I promise to always be there for you, whatever comes. I promise to be a good father if we are blessed with children. And I know it will be easy because loving you and being with you is the single greatest joy of my entire life."

She had to reach back and shake her hand so Jill would know she needed a tissue. They'd agreed on a signal before the wedding. As soon as it was delivered, he took it from her and dabbed at her tears, his whole heart in his eyes.

After taking a few deep breaths, she smiled and said, "Tanner, when I came to Dare Valley, I was looking for myself, for the woman I'd lost somewhere in New York. With Divorcee Woman's help, I found her. And I'm grateful for that. I want to come to you whole and complete."

He tilted his head to the side and gazed into her eyes, likely remembering just how lost she'd been. Her divorce had taken a toll on her, and it had forced her to take a hard look at both the woman she'd become and the woman she wanted to be.

"I returned to Dare Valley on a quest to prove fairy tales still exist like they do in Nora Roberts' books. But you taught me one very important thing. That a real hero is better than any storybook character, and true love is more incredible than any love story could ever describe. I love you with a heart that seems to have grown a thousand times bigger these last months. And even though I can't imagine loving you more than I do right now, I know I will as we work together and play together and have a family together here in Dare Valley. Thank you for loving me and accepting me as I am. I promise to love you the same way."

He pressed their foreheads together when she finished, and she could feel he was struggling with the strong emotion flowing between them. When he seemed more settled, he edged back and traced her face with his free hand.

"For always," he whispered.

"For always," she whispered back.

Then the minister blessed the rings, and it made her cry again to see Tanner slide her Grandma Harriet's ruby and diamond wedding ring onto her finger. She looked over her shoulder to see her grandpa wiping at the tears in his eyes. When he caught her looking, he gave her a thumbs-up, and she simply nodded over the tightness in her throat. Neither of them needed to give voice to the understanding that passed between them.

When the minister announced them husband and wife and said Tanner could kiss her, she threw her arms around his neck, making him laugh, and poured all her love into a simple kiss she knew she would remember all the days of her life.

And with his hand in hers, they walked down the aisle after their wedding party.

She had to fight the urge to throw her bouquet up in the air and cheer.

***

Tanner suffered through the wedding photos in the fabulous brass and marble rotunda in Emmits Merriam University's Main Administration building, but the minute they were over, he yanked off his boutonniere. It had been sticking into him for the last twenty minutes.

"Undressing already?" his bride asked with a saucy smile.

"I'm game, if you are," he answered in a voice only she could hear, caressing the hollow of her throat. He'd never imagined lace could be so sexy, and her dress was tantalizing him way too early.

"We have guests, if you'll remember," she said, stroking the lapels of his suit. So not helpful.

Asher ducked his head into their conversation. "Some of us have come from across the Atlantic to be here. You two had better not be thinking about ducking off before I dance with the bride."

"We are," Tanner said, right as she said, "We're not."
They grinned at each other.

Jill threaded her hand through Asher's arm. "Could he be any dreamier? I've said it all my life, and I'll say it again. *Everything* sounds better with a British accent. And to test my point, Asher, I want you to say a few words. Natalie! Caroline! Moira! Come here. You've gotta hear this."

His friend didn't roll his eyes—he was way too proper a British gentleman for that—but it was close. Her cousins clustered around them, all of them giving Asher an eyeful. Well, all but Natalie, who seemed about as interested in him as if he were an elderly relative of Tanner's.

"All right, Jill," Asher said politely. "What do you wish for me to say?"

"Say horse puckey," Jill ordered.

Asher's mouth twitched. "Horse puckey."

Jill fanned herself like she was breathless. Caroline and Moira deflated like day-old balloons.

"See. Now say maggot."

"Maggot."

The women's sighs were worthy of Sarah Bernhardt and her understudies.

"I knew it! Even the gross words sound sexy!" Jill declared with a stomp of her heel, which echoed in the vast rotunda.

"I'll be sure to tell all my television counterparts. Now how about we go find a glass of something delightfully alcoholic?"

"That sounds divine," Jill replied, sugar-coating it plenty.

Asher offered his other arm to Caroline, who took it with a simpering smile. Natalie and Moira followed the trio to the door that led to the reception area.

"If we hurry, we can find a closet somewhere and make out for a while," Tanner whispered into

Meredith's ear. "The coast is clear, but it won't stay that way for long."

Meredith entwined her hands around his neck and gave him a kiss that made even his stalwart knees go weak.

"You're killing me. Right here. And at our own wedding, no less." He tucked her closer to his body. "You wear some dress made all out of lace to drive me wild and God knows what kind of underwear underneath it all. Then you make me go to a church and stand in front of a minister and talk about how much I want you."

"You poor baby," she said in a sad, pouty tone that drove him wild.

"If that's not bad enough, I have to smell your perfume as we smile for the camera, knowing I have to eat a full-blown meal, cut a ridiculously tiered cake, and dance in front of everybody. And I have to do this all the while pretending I'm not aroused out of my mind, knowing I'm going to get lucky tonight. Do *any* of your wedding magazines cover the man's point of view? I might have to write an article on this."

He could warn other men what to expect and suggest they wear extra-long suit jackets to cover the evidence of their wedding-day longing.

"My underwear is all white, appropriately lacy, and has MW stitched into the top of the panties for Married Woman."

He'd given her cotton underwear with MW stitched into them as part of his marriage proposal. It might have been unconventional, but the time had come for her to let go of Divorcee Woman, the superwoman alter ego who had helped her regain confidence after her divorce.

"You're enjoying this, aren't you?"

She took a few steps toward the door to their reception hall, which was down the corridor, and then gave him a sexy look over her shoulder. "What do you think?"

There was no question. He was going to die a happy man tonight.

He followed her into the party and watched with a smile as she rushed straight into her grandfather's arms.

The reception area was the perfect place for two ink-blooded journalists to celebrate their marriage. Black-and-white photos of Arthur Hale and other award-winning journalists and world leaders graced the wood-paneled hall, as was appropriate since it was called The Arthur Hale Conference Center. The large windows provided sweeping vistas of the valley and the surrounding snow-covered mountains. But one of the most impressive features of the room, in Tanner's humble view, was the award case holding one of Arthur's Pulitzer Prizes at the back of the room. The others were in his office, which is where Tanner had decided to display his. Maybe when he won another one, he would give it to the journalism school for display.

Today the hall was filled with round tables decorated with amaryllis flowers and lit with tiny candles Tanner knew wouldn't last the evening. There was a dance floor area set up between the main tables and the head table. The open bar was at the back, and people were already helping themselves to drinks. Even though he'd seen the hall last night, the whole scene felt different today. It was everything he and Meredith had hoped for: warm and romantic.

Somehow, being surrounded by the journalistic integrity and excellence he loved so much, which his new family also lived and breathed, seemed to forge an even stronger connection between him and Meredith on the first day of their married life.

"I love it here," Asher said as Tanner moved further into the room. "I might have to teach here as an adjunct one day—like you did. This is like coming to journalistic heaven. Did you see that photo of your new grandfather-in-law, if there's such a word, with Anwar Sadat and Jimmy Carter in the 1970s?"

"I did. Arthur is truly one of the most incredible men you will ever meet. You seem to have lost your admirers," he said with a playful nudge to his friend's ribs.

"I said I had to go to the loo. It's degrading. Those women are animals," Asher joked. "Especially your new sister-in-law. I feel like some English boy toy. Fortunately she only has eyes for one man, and he came and stole her away." He nodded toward his left.

Tanner looked over to where Jill and Brian were talking while sipping what looked to be beer. The two were renewing their friendship at the moment, and she'd asked him to be her date to the wedding. It was a start.

"She's been in love with him since she was a little girl," he told Asher. "He's been...a bit more obtuse about the whole thing."

"Punch him if he breaks her heart," Asher said, unbuttoning his tailored Savile Row suit.

"I will," he said easily. "He knows he needs to handle her with care."

"She's a spunky one," Asher said, picking up a glass of champagne from one of the trays the servers were walking through the room. "Now, tell me what it's like to work with Arthur day in and day out."

They started talking shop, something Tanner had missed doing. He loved working at *The Western Independent,* but he was still adjusting to not covering the news in the field. By the time the conversation had turned to the ongoing conflict in the Middle East, Meredith came over.

"It's time for us to find our seats so the waiters can start serving everybody," she said, taking his hand.

Sure enough, everyone had begun to find their

tables. It felt wonderful to see all these people who were special to him and Meredith melded together in one place.

Dinner was much better than he'd expected, and when he told Meredith, she laughed and said never to underestimate a Hale. Her cousin, Natalie, had done a great job with the beef tenderloin. Meredith had pretty much ploughed through the entire salmon on her plate.

"Were you a little hungry?" he teased, leaning over to kiss her cheek.

"Starved. Getting married burns a lot of calories."

Since Jill was sitting on Meredith's side, and she would hardly be offended if she overheard, he leaned in and whispered, "If you think that's a lot of calories, wait until tonight."

She laughed huskily. "I'll have Natalie make us a to-go bag."

"Good idea. I love you for being as smart as you are sexy."

"You're a big talker."

He picked up his beer. "Yes, I am, but I always deliver."

When it came time to cut their cake—a two-tiered, square, dark chocolate confection with mocha almond cream and an M and T cake topper—he made sure to be nice and feed her small bites so he wouldn't mess up her makeup. She wasn't so nice, using a finger to spread the buttercream frosting down the dent in his chin. Some of their guests started cheering. Asher used his Cairo-cab-calling whistle, which could shatter glass. Before he could complain, she stood on her tiptoes and kissed it off his chin, sending lust coursing through his system as fast as the sugar was. Before it got too out of hand, he gave her a hard kiss and grabbed a napkin to wipe the rest off.

Then the DJ was cued up, and they danced to the song he'd chosen: Billy Joel's "Just The Way You Are."

There was something about that song.

He twirled her around, loving how she laughed and sashayed to the beat. Then he handed her off to her dad and grabbed Jill for a dance. When he glanced at his sister and lifted his head as if to say, *Do you want to dance?* Peggy shook her head and nudged Keith onto the dance floor. His nephew ran over to him, so he spent the next dance teaching him how to wiggle his hips to "Sweet Caroline."

Then he took his turns with Meredith's mom, her cousins, and her aunt—and all of them confirmed what he knew about Hale women—whether by blood or marriage. None of them liked the man to lead. He mentioned that to Meredith when she finally came back into his arms.

"Something to remember," she told him with a husky laugh. "You knew what you were getting into when you asked me to marry you."

He gave her what he hoped was a dashing smile, one that would make her knees as weak as his were after dancing with her pressed against him.

"Promise me our daughters will be the same way," he whispered.

Her eyes immediately teared up, and he puffed out his chest, proud of himself. The night was almost over, and he finally felt like he was unlocking all the secrets for the perfect wedding day. The bride was supposed to arouse the groom to distraction while the groom was supposed to make the bride get all misty-eyed.

"I promise our daughters will be the same way," she said with a special light in her green eyes.

Then he took her mouth in a deep kiss to show her just how eager he was to get to work on her promise.

***

Meredith was having so much fun, she didn't want

the night to end. Sure, her feet hurt from dancing too much in her heels. And some of her hair had long since fallen out of her formerly perfect coif. But none of that mattered. She'd married the man of her dreams and was having the time of her life with her family and friends.

Asher spun her around on the dance floor, and heavens did that man have moves. She had to admit there was something charming and very sexy about him, which she could admire as a happily married woman.

"I'm so glad you could make it, Asher," she said as the song came to an end. "It meant the world to Tanner, and I'm so happy I finally got to meet you."

"Me too," he told her. "Now I understand how Tanner could give up the adventuresome life of a war correspondent to settle down in Dare Valley. You make him happier than I've ever seen him."

"He makes me feel the same way," she replied, lifting a foot off the ground and giving her arch a little stretch.

"Who makes you happy?" her groom asked, putting his hand on her waist from behind.

She settled her back against his chest. "You do."

"Good answer. Are you ready for me to tell the DJ to play the last dance? I want to get out of here."

Asher chuckled, and Meredith felt her face heat as her mind jumped to their wedding night. She'd been fantasizing about it for weeks now.

"I want one more dance with someone special," she told him with a smile. "Then you can tell the DJ."

He kissed her cheek, and she could tell he knew what she meant. "Okay. Make it a good one."

She headed directly toward her grandpa. He was seated at a table on the edge of the makeshift dance floor with her parents. She'd asked him to dance earlier in the night, but he'd blustered something fierce about being too old, so she'd backed down. This time she wasn't taking no for an answer.

Planting her hands on her hips, she stared him down. "You're dancing with me. Grab your cane. Does Frank Sinatra work for you?"

He frowned, but he picked up his cane and stood, rubbing his hip. "I told you before. I'm too old to dance with you young people."

"You danced with Joanie," she said as she gave the DJ the signal they'd agreed on earlier.

"Fly Me To The Moon" began to play, and they walked to the center of the dance floor. Her parents followed them and started dancing cheek-to-cheek. She was happy to see Jill rest her head on Brian's shoulder.

"Joanie is my date. Plus, she and I run at the same speed," her grandpa said, still glowering. "I can't shake and wiggle to all that junk you young people listen to."

Since he was being his usual blustery self, she merely kissed his weathered jaw. "I don't expect you to shake and wiggle to Sinatra."

"Good," he harrumphed. "It isn't dignified."

Even with his cane, he was a better lead than most men, having been raised in a generation where men knew how to dance with women. She made her muscles go soft as he led her through a basic waltz.

"Grandpa?" she asked. "What's the secret to a happy marriage? Like you and Grandma Harriet had?"

His breath rushed out. "If your grandma were still here, she'd say the same thing I'm about to say to you. Love. I know that sounds way too simple, but it's the God's honest truth. So long as you cultivate that love, you're good to go."

She rested her head on his shoulder, making sure to match his slow but confident steps. "Any suggestions on how to cultivate it?"

"Marriage is like putting a newspaper together," he told her, making her smile.

Leave it to Arthur Hale to use a journalism metaphor.

"You have to remain curious about your partner. You have to keep asking questions. And when something doesn't add up, you have to dig deeper. Then it's all a matter of choosing the right words, and when you use the wrong ones—either in an argument or because you've had a rough day—you have to print a retraction."

"Any other sage advice?" she said with a grin.

"Trust your gut. Pay attention to the details. Search for the right words. And never, ever take him or what his story is for granted." He kissed the top of her head. "And look through keyholes if you need to."

She laughed. That was one of the journalistic rules he'd taught her growing up. Some of them he'd meant. Others had been for fun. Through it all, he'd opened up the world for her by feeding the passion they both shared.

"I love you, Grandpa," she said, inhaling his familiar scent of Old Spice and red hots.

He stopped dancing, and they came to a halt.

"I love you too, Mermaid. Now go find your husband so you can dance the last dance together. If he feels anything like I did on my wedding day to your grandmother, he can't wait to get the hell out of here."

Even though she knew he'd bluster, she pinched his cheek. "You are the dearest man I know."

He looked up, as if asking heaven for help. "Go on with you."

With a little nudge, she set off to find Tanner, who was still talking to Asher.

"Are you finally ready for the last dance?" she asked with the slight tilt of her head, which she hoped looked seductive.

"You have to ask?" He was so eager to get onto the dance floor, she had to run to keep up.

The DJ cued up "It Had To Be You," and Tanner pulled her close, so close she could feel his body heat pouring through his suit.

"You *are* anxious to leave."

"I've been trying to tell you that for hours," he said in a huskier voice than usual.

"I asked Grandpa to tell me the keys to a happy marriage." Tanner's dark eyes never left her face as she relayed what he'd said.

When she finished, he said, "I'm not worried about it."

Even though she wasn't either, she asked, "You're not?"

His smile was devilish and charming at the same time. "No. If marriage is anything like running a newspaper, I plan on winning a Pulitzer."

And as he swept her up into his arms, she whispered in his ear, "Me too."

JILL & BRIAN

When Jill Hale had imagined her wedding as a child, she'd envisioned hundreds of friends and families seated in purple velvet chairs under a pink circus tent, the smell of lemonade ices perfuming the air as she married her best friend, Brian McConnell. The morning of her wedding would be magical and straight out of a storybook, just as it should be for a princess.

As she entered her teenage years, her vision changed, and her dream wedding took on an earthier feel. The large gathering would take place in one of the mountainous valleys surrounding her hometown, just as the wildflowers popped open. Then she and Brian had a picnic in just such a bucolic valley with their best friends, Jemma and Pete, and were swarmed by an avalanche of bugs, which put an early end to that notion.

After Brian McConnell broke her heart and took off to New York City after high school to become a chef, her big day changed yet again, turning edgier. She would marry an artist with shaggy long hair who liked to write her poetry. A love priestess would bless their union with wild sage incense and ribbons the same colors of each chakra energy center in her and her partner's bodies.

Now, at twenty-six, she was finally getting married, and her plans didn't match any of her earlier visions.

Truth be told, she *wasn't* having a large wedding, and though she'd looked into the pink circus tent out of curiosity, it turned out they were nearly impossible to rent, least of all to assemble. She *wasn't* having it in a valley dotted with wildflowers—even if they could have sprayed for bugs, it was too cold on this early May day. And she *wasn't* marrying a hippie artist to match her own creative self.

But she *was* marrying Brian McConnell, her best friend from childhood *and* the love of her life, and when it came down to it, nothing was more important.

They were getting married on a Friday, which was the only day they could book their local pastor on short notice. Speed was a must because she and Brian had accidentally made a bun in the oven way before they were ready. But they were finally in love. Correction. Brian was finally in love with her. That blockhead had made her wait nearly her whole life, but now that he'd found his brain like the Scarecrow Groom he was, she didn't care.

She was mostly over the moon about the baby now—except for the puking part—but having a baby had prompted a different approach to wedding planning.

It was like they'd ordered the fast-food wedding special—even though Brian hated it when she called it that. He was such a gourmet food snob sometimes. But she wasn't complaining. She'd dreamed about marrying Brian McConnell since the third grade. Now she was going to have him for good.

But everything had been so hectic lately, what with her new "Love"—emphasis on the capital L—relationship with Brian, the BABY—who deserved all caps—her new job with The Grand Mountain Hotel, and training Margie to be the new manager of her coffee shop, Don't Soy With Me. And that was why she was currently locked in her sister Meredith's bathroom while her mom, her sister, her Denver cousins, and her dear friend, Peggy McBride, chatted outside. They were laughing about something, and she felt a little left out, but it felt good to take this quick moment for herself.

"Jill!" Meredith called. "Did you fall in or something? Come on, we need to get to the church pretty soon."

Her makeup was flawless, she had to admit, and it did a great job of covering the red splotches on her face from an early-morning bout of morning sickness. She hadn't put on her dress yet or her shoes. She prayed no one would notice that the bride wore a size eleven heel. Please God let them be too busy gazing in wonder at the most beautiful bride they'd ever seen. Her. She could finally look in the mirror and see her beauty. Brian had helped with that, but she'd mostly done it herself.

Her red hair lay in curled waves down her back. Putting it up in some coif wouldn't have been her, and no one would have recognized her in the pictures. The pink blush on her cheeks made the hollows look a little more pronounced, like she had more prominent cheekbones. And her signature Hale green eyes—well she wasn't too shy to admit they looked like sparkling emeralds.

"You'd better call a plumber," she called back. "My engagement ring fell off my finger when I was flushing, and it went down the toilet."

"*What?*" her sister and a few of her cousins called out.

She opened the door with a smirk and held her left hand up so her ring glinted in the light. "Gotcha!"

Her mother, Linda, fanned herself. "Jill Marie Hale. I swear. Sometimes you give me heart palpitations."

Since Jill's dad had recently experienced heart palpitations and then some, her smirk faded. "Sorry,

Mom. I was just responding to what Meredith said about me falling in. Jeez. Can't anyone go to the bathroom in peace anymore?"

"You were in there forever," Meredith said.

"Natalie," she said to her cousin, "was she timing me?"

The brunette tapped her watch face. "No, but I was. Jill, you told me to keep you on schedule. You said, and I repeat, 'You know how I am.'"

Which is why Natalie was always in charge of the wedding emergency kit at family weddings. Unlike a normal kit with red-eye drops or moist towelettes, hers included saltine crackers and sparkling water, which always settled her stomach.

"Good point." She *did* know how she was. If there had been a high school yearbook category for the Woman Who Will Most Probably Be Late For Her Own Wedding, she would have swept it. She had always been way too spontaneous for her own good.

"Let's get a move on then," her cousin, Moira, said, picking up the plastic garment bag holding her dress. "I have the dress."

"I have the makeup bag," her other cousin, Caroline, said.

Her mom rushed up and gave her a big hug. "And I have you, Jillie Bean."

Meredith bustled in and hugged them both. "Me too."

Seconds later, her cousins joined in, and it was a giant hug fest. When they pulled apart, Peggy McBride's face was pinched tight since Jill had pulled her in. Okay, more like dragged her in.

"This is a little too much girl bonding for me."

"Well, you are the deputy sheriff of this town," Jill said to pacify her discomfort. "You don't want to ruin your rep."

"Let's go," Meredith said, picking up her purse and

Jill's overnight bag.

She and Brian had spent the previous night apart so that they could reflect on how far they'd come together before the big day. And of course...as Brian had said in a husky tone, so they could both imagine the wedding night. It was still pretty weird to be horny and pregnant, she had to admit, but she was willing to get used to it. With a cherry on top, she might add.

They hustled out of the girls-only house. All men had been banned the previous night for a Hale sleepover. Even poor Tanner and his and Meredith's dog, Hugo, since he technically had a weenie.

To Jill's horror, Brian's SUV came rumbling down the driveway just as she was opening the passenger side of her sister's car.

"Groom alert!" Meredith called out.

The women started to shriek. Peggy even ran toward the SUV with her hands held out like a traffic cop's, prepared to stop him with her flinty cop look.

That didn't deter Brian. No, he cut the engine and hopped out.

"Hello, ladies," he drawled, acting like he wasn't breaking the biggest rule on the planet.

"Get back in the car, McConnell," Peggy said in her meanest voice ever, "before I cuff you and take you downtown—to the church where you belong."

"Yeah, Brian," Moira said, hiding the wedding dress, which thankfully could not be seen through the garment bag. "Shoo."

He laughed and headed directly toward Jill. She knew that look. He wasn't going to be stopped, not even by the hen house he now faced.

"What are you doing here?" she asked in total exasperation. "You aren't supposed to see me before the wedding."

"I'm not supposed to see you in your wedding dress," he told her. "I looked up the rules."

She rolled her eyes. "This had better be good."

His brow arched, and his smile grew to a grin akin to the one sported by a certain Cheshire cat. "What faith you have in me. I worried you might panic and think I was calling things off. I'm in awe of you, Red."

Her heart did swell a little at his praise. He was right. It was a big deal that her mind hadn't instantly turned Negative Nancy at the sight of his SUV. "I believe in us. I know you do too. Finally."

"I'll ignore that crack about me being slow since it's our wedding day." He stepped forward and laid his hand on her belly. "But I have a slight correction. I believe in *all* of us. Now, take a ride with me."

If not for the look in his eyes and the gentle touch he spared for the baby growing inside her, she might have shooed him off. But he had a purpose for being here—a sweet one, it seemed—and this was her day. Besides, wasn't she known for being spontaneous?

"Ladies," she called out, taking his hand. "Brian will see me to the church after we take a drive. I'll meet you there."

"Brian McConnell!" her mom called out. "If you are taking my daughter off for a pre-wedding quickie, I will box your ears."

Few people could make a grown man blush like Linda Hale. "Jeez, Mrs. Hale, I'm not...cripes...I'd never."

"Good," her mom said. "And please call me Linda, dear. You're not ten years old anymore."

As they walked to his car, Jill leaned in to murmur, "No, you sure aren't, thank God. I believe you've grown out in all the right areas."

His thumb rubbed the back of her hand. "Yeah, I rather like being taller than you. For a few years there, you made me feel like a midget."

"You should have experienced it from my perspective. I was fourteen and five ten while all of you boys topped out at five seven. It made school dances a true horror."

"But I still danced with you anyway." He opened the car door for her.

"Not that you could dance," she said with a knowing wink, referring to the dance lessons she'd tried to give him.

"I'll ignore that and finish my sentence. I was about to say that I always will. Dance with you, that is."

"Ah," she said, pretending to wipe a tear from her eye.

When he drove into town and pulled up in front of the cemetery, she didn't have to pretend to wipe the tears running down her face. He helped her do that with a gentle finger as tears shined in his own Bengal-tiger-blue eyes.

"I thought we should have Jemma with us today since…" he said, trailing off to clear his throat.

Her eyes scanned across the graveyard to find her best friend's grave. When Jemma had died nearly eight months ago of a heart murmur, her own heart had been yanked out and flattened by a fleet of tractor trailers on the highway.

"Since she couldn't come," she finished for him, her own voice as hoarse as his. "You really are the sweetest man alive. Have I told you that today?"

He wrapped her up in his arms. "No, but feel free to say it every day. I have a feeling we're going to need some reminding. All right. Now, let's go see our friend."

When he came around to her car door and helped her out, he snagged a bouquet of pink roses from the back. Jill sniffed when she saw them and then reached for his hand. Pain pinching her heart, she walked with him through the gray markers of death.

***

Brian hadn't expected to feel grief squeeze his chest on his wedding day, but he hadn't stopped thinking about all the good old times he'd shared with Jill. Which had led him to think about their two best friends growing up: Jemma and Pete. As kids, they'd always been known as the Four Musketeers. They had bonded on the first day of kindergarten after toilet papering the schoolroom together because it was...well, impossible to resist the pink and blue toilet paper in the boys' and girls' bathrooms.

The school had switched to standard toilet paper soon after, but that had only been the start of a long career as practical jokers. The Four Musketeers went on to hang purple pens on pink ribbons from the florescent light fixtures in third grade. In seventh grade, they smuggled a dozen pink plastic flamingos into their classroom. And when they were sophomores in high school, they freed dozens of frogs destined for the cutting block in biology class after Jill and Jemma's protests of animal cruelty were ignored by the administration.

Now, Jemma was gone way too soon. And Pete...well, they weren't very good friends anymore. Pete had left town after Jemma's death, needing to escape the weight of old memories, and they hadn't spoken since.

"Pete's been here," Jill said when they stopped in front of Jemma's grave.

Sure enough, a mixed bouquet of flowers—the same type Pete had always bought for Jemma when they were dating—lay against the gravestone. Brian traced Jemma's name and the angel carved above it. "Yes, and they're fresh."

Did that mean Pete had decided to come to their wedding, after all? After some discussion, Jill had agreed to extend a peace offering and invite him, but they hadn't heard back.

"Maybe he'll come," he told her, squeezing her hand.

They'd both lost their best friends in different ways, and the hurt of it had rocked them to the core. Now, all they had were each other and this new family they were making together—and the wacky Hale family, of course.

"I...wish Jem was here," he whispered, his throat tight with emotion.

"Me too," Jill said, brushing away more tears. "I always thought she'd be standing at the altar with me."

Pete was supposed to have been his groomsman, but that hadn't worked out either. He pulled her into his arms as she cried, and rocked them both. Then he felt a spot of warmth on his back, almost like Jemma's comforting hand was resting there. Part of him thought he might be a little crazy, but he'd visited her here often, and he'd sensed it before. She *was* there. Or something of her was. And it soothed him like always.

"She's here," he said in a soft tone against her neck. "Can't you feel her?"

She inhaled jaggedly and nodded. "Yes. When the baby gets big enough inside me, I want to come back and visit her. I...I just know the baby is going to kick...almost as if he or she can feel her too."

Talking about the baby kicking—the miracle they hadn't meant to make—was pretty much enough to turn him to pudding. "Do you have any idea how much I love you? How precious you and the baby are to me? Jill....Jill...I'm so damn happy we're together."

The laugh she uttered was a bit desperate with emotion. "Finally. I love you too. And you and the baby...well, it's going to be awesome."

It hadn't started out that way. He'd been shocked and more than a little freaked out at first. He hadn't expected to make a baby before he was thirty, and certainly not before he was married, but sometimes fate knew better. Both he and Jill had pretty hard heads, so perhaps they'd needed a kick to their proverbial behinds.

Jill pressed back and traced the top of Jemma's grave. "I miss you, Jem. So much. I wish you could see my dress. Heck, I wish you could have been with me and my family when we bought it. I wish you could have been at my bachelorette party. I wish…"

He reached for her hand again.

"I wish you were still here, dammit."

"That's my wish too," he said. "But I have to believe she'll find a way to be there."

His beautiful bride-to-be turned her head to gaze at him. She stopped his very breath, made his heart rate lull to a slow, thudding beat.

"Like heavenvision instead of television?" she asked.

"Or she could just be a ghost like in *Charmed*. She loved that show."

"We both did."

The silence grew around them. The wind rushed up and over them suddenly, sending the tree limbs into a playful dance, like the leaves were waving at them. And damn if the sun didn't peek out from behind a cloud and shine on them with blinding light.

"Yeah, I think she's here," Jill said quietly. "Let's go get married, Bri."

He turned her to him and chucked her under the chin, something he used to do when he was flirting with her in high school. "I thought you'd never ask."

Just like he was expecting, she poked him in the belly. They laughed a little, which eased their grief. And as they walked through the sunshine, heading back to the church to say their vows, they both felt a warmth on their backs and knew Jemma walked with them.

***

Jill took a moment to admire her dress in the full-length mirror of the church bridal room. Her dress wasn't white—and not because she was knocked up. Nope. She'd meant to wear white, but that was before she'd seen this yellow wedding dress tucked away on a rack in the corner of the wedding shop with a sign above it saying *For the Daring Bride*. She hadn't been able to resist. Color. It was her best friend.

While the sunshine tone might be too daring for some, the dress itself was simple, suiting her tastes. The chiffon skirt fell to the ground in a sumptuous line while the bodice's material crisscrossed over her breasts and then curled over her shoulders. She'd chosen a simple wedding flower crown rather than a traditional veil. The white cherry blossoms contrasted beautifully with her red hair and gave her the dreamy elegance of a flower child bride, something she rather liked.

"You look beautiful, Jill," Meredith said from beside her.

The rest of her family echoed her sister's comment, oohing and ahhing over her.

Everyone had understood the reason for her spontaneous drive after hearing that Brian had taken her to visit Jemma's grave. They'd all loved Jemma, so a few of them had teared up too.

"You look pretty darn beautiful too," she said back to her sister, running her hands down the silky fabric of her dress. It rippled when she sashayed in place, and the fabric felt luxurious against her thigh-high-stocking-clad legs, which were going to drive Brian crazy later.

"I never thought I would look good in purple," Meredith said, pointing down at her dress, "but this shade is actually quite lovely."

"Like you would have gone for a deep purple. I knew I needed to keep it romantic. Violet seemed appropriate." And the dress was a simple A-line, in keeping with her and Brian's wish to go a little more casual.

Except in the food department. She was marrying a

chef, after all.

Everyone else was dressed in simple, flowing dresses—some silk, some chiffon—in bold colors suiting her Hale cousins' style. Okay, everyone except for Peggy, who was wearing a navy pantsuit. Jill's mom was wearing a lovely violet mother-of-the-bride dress with white pearls beaded across the scoop neckline.

"I have something for you," Meredith said, reaching into her blue overnight bag. "It might make you cry, but we can always re-do your makeup."

She braced herself as Meredith pulled out a black jewelry box. "What is it?"

Her sister opened it with a click. "I know how much you wanted Jemma here, and so did her mom. She wanted you to wear Jemma's pearl earrings. They're part of your wedding present from her family."

Her lip wobbled, and sure enough, a couple of fat tears trailed down her face as she stared at those luminescent pearls. "Oh, my. That was so sweet of her." She remembered Jemma receiving those pearls for her sixteenth birthday. They'd been her favorite accessory that summer.

She took them out and fitted them into her ear lobes, handling them delicately. They seemed to glow, and she felt that same warmth on her back she'd experienced in the graveyard. Taking a deep breath, she pointed to her own overnight bag.

"Hand that to me, please," she asked her sister.

When Meredith did, she dug inside for the black box holding the necklace she'd decided to wear. She hadn't told Brian, but she knew it would mean the world to him. She opened the box. For her high school graduation present, he'd bought her a simple gold heart necklace with *J&B, BFFs* engraved on the back. It wasn't fancy, but it was exactly what she wanted to wear, and it felt so right to pair it with Jemma's pearl earrings.

"Brian is going to be moved when he sees that

necklace, honey," her mom said, putting her arm around her waist. "I'm so proud of you two. Nothing could make me happier than seeing the two of you get married."

"Not to mention the fact that you're gaga for your future grandchild," Jill responded with a knowing wink.

Her mom raised her hands. "Guilty."

"I wish Grandma Harriet could see me today," Jill said, thinking about the wonderful woman who'd made her cookies and supported her dream to go into business on her own, leaving her with the money to pursue just such a path when she passed away.

"She is, honey," her mom said, "right along with Jemma."

She sniffed, and Natalie—ever vigilant in her wedding emergency kit duties—handed her a tissue. Wiping her eyes, she took one last look in the mirror and then glanced at the clock on the wall. Ten till five.

"I'm getting married in ten minutes," she whispered, feeling a strange sense of unreality wash over her. Sometimes it was so hard to believe all her dreams were finally coming true.

A knock sounded on the door. Her mom went to answer it.

"Oh, Jillie Bean," her dad said, stepping inside. "You look beautiful, sweetheart. Simply beautiful."

She walked over and kissed Alan Hale's cheek. "Thanks, Dad."

"You girls better go find your seats," he told them, chucking Moira under the chin as she and her sisters fanned out.

"We'll see you out there," Peggy said with a distinct nod.

Her mom kissed her cheek before following the others. "I better go find my seat too. Alan, you take care of our girls."

Just after her mom stepped out of the room, Jill

heard the unmistakable tap of a cane on the floor. She looked over, and sure enough, Grandpa Hale came inside.

"I thought I'd pop in and kiss the bride before all the shenanigans started," he said.

Leave it to her grandpa to refer to a wedding that way. She was already smiling as she kissed his cheek.

"I'm so glad you came back here, Grandpa," she told him. "I was missing Grandma just now."

He coughed. "My mind was in the same place. She would have loved to see you getting married, especially to Brian. She had this inkling you two would end up together, even when he left Dare Valley and broke your heart."

She pressed a hand to her heart. "I didn't know she felt that way."

"She was a wise woman," he told her. "She didn't think you'd appreciate her saying that, given how angry you were at Brian back then. Now, he and I are business partners in his new restaurant. She would have loved that."

"I love it too," she said, straightening the boutonniere on his gray suit. "You look pretty handsome for an old rascal."

"You look pretty good yourself," he said with a wink.

The music from the church organ filtered back to them, signaling the start of the wedding. Grandpa blew them a kiss and headed off to find his seat. Jill faced her dad and sister.

"Okay, let's do this."

Meredith gathered her bouquet from the table and took her position in the back of the church, waiting for the cue in the music to begin her walk down the aisle. Jill reached for her own bouquet. The simple arrangement of lavender roses, purple peonies, and white Stephanotis was stunning against the buttery tones of her dress. Plus, the purple made her happy.

"Are you ready, kiddo?" her dad asked when the music she and Brian had chosen started to play.

"The Wedding March" hadn't been their style, so they'd settled on "Marry Me" by Train. The sound of the instrumental version conducted by the local band they'd hired was enough to bring tears to her eyes.

"I'm ready," she whispered and threaded her arm through his.

As she walked down the aisle, she held her head high and looked at Brian. He was so handsome in a heather gray tux with a purple vest and necktie. His boutonniere was a simple lavender rose. His Bengal-tiger-blue eyes gleamed the closer she came, heavy with longing and love.

She didn't have eyes for anyone but him, and it took her a moment to realize her dad was turning her and kissing her on the cheek.

"I love you, Jillie," he whispered.

"I love you too, Dad," she whispered back.

She stepped away from her dad, toward Brian.

Toward her new life.

***

Brian held out his hand to her, his heart thundering in his chest, and Jill clasped it tightly after handing Meredith her bouquet.

"You are the most beautiful woman I've ever seen," he said softly.

Her mouth curved. "Thanks. You look pretty handsome yourself."

"Are you ready for this?" he asked, gazing down at her dress. Yellow was so perfect for her. She hadn't said a word to him about her decision to go with something other than white, but it suited her to a tee.

"I've been ready for years," she said in a near whisper.

"Thanks for waiting for me to catch on," he responded just as quietly.

And with that they turned to the minister, ready to make the final commitment.

He couldn't look away from her. Her long red hair curled beautifully around her shoulders, and the flower thingee in her hair made her seem younger and more vulnerable. It reminded him of how she'd looked in high school, back when he'd been too scared to ask her to go out with him for real.

Perhaps they would have gotten together years ago if he'd been braver, but he planned to more than make up for the time they'd lost.

He bowed his head as a new reverence came over him. Declaring his love for her in front of their family and friends was a little nerve-racking, but it felt so right to make this commitment in front of her parents, who were clasping each other's hands so tightly in the front row. His now-divorced parents had come and were seated rows apart, and seeing them again had been as strained and awkward as always. In some ways, Jill's mom and dad felt more like parents to him than his own messed up family did, which was one reason he'd spent so much time over at their house as a kid—the other being Jill. Jill's mom had taught him to cook, fostered his interest and ability in all things food, and helped him dream he could be a chef. He was so proud to be a permanent member of the Hale clan.

When she said her vows, her voice broke, and he dug out the handkerchief Arthur Hale had given him before the wedding, saying a wise groom was a prepared groom. Rather than hand her the silk cloth, he wiped the tears away gently himself, and the tenderness made more tears fall. She might be tough, but she needed tenderness too.

When it came time for him to say his vows, he had to clear his voice a couple of times over the thickening in his throat. He'd practiced them at least ten times, but they held new meaning in this moment, when her face was glowing with so much love he thought his heart would burst.

"I, Brian McConnell, take you, Jill Hale, to be my wife, my best friend, and my partner from this day forward. In the presence of God and our family and friends, I offer you my solemn vow to support you in sickness and in health, in good times and in bad, and in joy as well as in sorrow. I promise to love you unconditionally..."

She let out a shaky breath, and he had to release the air trapped in his lungs.

"To support you in your goals, to honor and respect you, to laugh with you and cry with you, and to cherish you for as long as we both shall live."

Her hands squeezed his, and he leaned forward spontaneously until he could whisper in her ear, "And I promise not to be a jerk from here on out and to be the best daddy to the baby we've made."

"Oh, Bri," she whispered back. "And I promise to be the best mommy too and not to be such a drama queen sometimes."

Now that made him laugh. "Only sometimes?"

She twisted his thumb a second, her shoulders shaking. "Life isn't fun if it's devoid of all drama."

"If you say so, Red," he said. The minister cleared his throat, a not-so-subtle reminder that they were veering off point.

When it came time for them to exchange rings, he slid the simple wedding band on her finger. He was in the process of opening his own restaurant, so he hadn't been able to afford anything grand. It embarrassed him, particularly since he wanted to present her with the world on a silver platter. She'd dismissed his apologies with her usual flair, saying she wasn't all about the flash. But he'd promised himself he would buy her something nicer once his restaurant became super successful, something he knew would happen.

Then he glanced up from her hand and noticed she was wearing the necklace he'd given her when they were eighteen, right after one of the worst fights of their life. It was the very fight that had shut her away from him for so many years. She looked so dazzling in her yellow gown that he'd somehow missed that tiny detail.

"You wore the necklace?" he whispered.

"Of course," she whispered back like he'd asked the dumbest question possible.

"I love you, Jill," he whispered, and the minister cleared his throat *again*.

When the minister finally declared them husband and wife and said it was time to kiss the bride, Brian was more than ready to do just that. Jill leaned into him, and he cuddled her close, aware of their baby growing bigger and bigger in her belly, even though it was probably the size of a pea right now.

He pressed his lips to hers, and she met him with fervor. The kiss must have lasted a bit longer than it was supposed to because soon the stupid minister was clearing his throat again. They were both laughing when they finally pulled away.

"Hello, wife," he said, grinning from ear to ear.

"Hello, husband," she said, beaming right back at him. "Now let's go eat. I'm hungry."

And with those words, they strode down the aisle hand in hand to the song Jill had insisted upon: "Happy Together" by The Turtles.

As they came to the last row, Jill let out a whoop. "We finally did it."

Yes, he thought, they finally had.

He caught sight of Pete standing in the back pew. Their eyes locked, and his old friend inclined his chin in greeting. Brian returned the gesture, his heart squeezing. Then Jill was pulling him out of the church, laughing with abandon, and he had no choice but to follow.

Not that he would have resisted.

He'd follow her pretty much anywhere she wanted to go.

***

Surveying the reception, Jill was happy to see that their limited budget was far from obvious. Simple chalkboard signs with romantic sayings had been placed all around the church reception hall, creating the kind of fun, sappy mood they'd wanted. Okay, that *she* had wanted. Brian had gone along with it. One of the sayings caught her eye, and she actually teared up. *Today I married my best friend.* Yeah, she sure had.

The beer barrow was inspired—she didn't care what anyone said. How fun was it to line a standard wheelbarrow with a bunch of microbrews? Not that she'd be drinking today. She wistfully eyed the espresso bar they'd set up for guests, manned by Margie Lancaster, her long-time friend and the new manager of Don't Soy With Me. She'd designed two special drinks for the reception: a wicked raspberry mocha with whipped cream and dark chocolate shavings and a salted caramel latte that would make most people beg for more. Except for Grandpa Hale, who would inevitably make some crack about serving frou-frou coffee drinks at her own wedding.

Brian came up behind her and put his hand around her waist. "Sorry I disappeared. I was trying to find Pete."

She'd seen their friend and felt...rather hollow. "I'm glad he came for you."

He kissed her cheek. "He came for both of us. And that was a nice peace offering if you ask me."

Her feelings toward Pete were more complicated

now that Jemma was gone, so she only hummed in her throat. "Are you happy with the food? I know you popped into the kitchen to check on things."

"I couldn't help myself, but you'll be happy to know I made sure to tug on an apron."

She fingered the lapel of his jacket. "Be a shame to have this ruined with an oil stain."

His brow rose. "Like you haven't thought about helping Margie at our espresso bar."

She had, but Margie would have pushed her off anyway. "She has everything under control."

"Um-hum," he said agreeably. "Let's go take these pictures so we can start the party."

The pictures were mostly annoying. Trying to get a picture where everyone was smiling was next to impossible, but Uncle Arthur kept cracking jokes, so it turned out to be more fun than expected.

When they finally re-entered the reception area, their guests were milling around the coffee station and makeshift bar. A huge cheer went up, and Jill felt herself flush at the attention. She was probably breaking out into spots, but hopefully her photographer would be able to Photoshop them out. They wove through the crowd, accepting hugs and kisses and congratulations. By the time Brian finally led her to the head table, she was starving.

"I'll be right back," he said, leaning down to kiss her neck, and she shook her head as he walked off toward the kitchen.

Their custom mugs made her smile. Hers said Mrs. Dancing Queen and his said Mr. Dream Chef.

She turned to Meredith, who was already seated by her. "He just can't help himself."

Her sister laughed. "He's in love. Savor it."

Moments later, Brian brought out a plate of food for her and set it in front of her in grand style. In the corner of her plate, he'd written *My Wife* in the red pepper sauce he'd chosen for the beef entrée. She rested her head on his shoulder when he sat down beside her.

"You're going to spoil me," she said softly.

He rested his hand on her thigh under the table. "It's a long night, and I've only just begun."

Her insides heated. "Then I'd better make sure I have enough fuel."

A server brought Brian his plate. "Dig in, Red. Everyone else is being served."

The beef tenderloin Brian had been able to negotiate for a wonderful price tickled her nose. The haricot verts were bright green and dotted with slivered almonds. And of course, he'd chosen to pair them with a potato gratin with gruyere cheese.

"This smells like heaven." She attacked her meal and didn't look back. After all, she was eating for two now.

When it came time for the toasts, Meredith proved she was the best sister on the planet by standing up and saying, "Everyone wants to marry their best friend. Jill and Brian were closer than any two people I knew growing up. I'm so happy they've decided to share their lives together. And Brian—even though you have always been part of the Hale family—I want to give you an official welcome anyway. To Jill and Brian."

The guests raised their champagne. She raised her sparkling water. And so the toasts continued until it was time to dance.

Jill had insisted that she be the one to select and communicate with the DJ, and Brian had been suspicious of her motives all week. She'd talked him into "You're My Best Friend" by Queen for their first dance since he wouldn't have to do much more than sway. He was still resisting her efforts to turn him into a Mr. Dancing King.

He took her in his arms and stared into her eyes, and she simply felt her heart fall at his feet.

"I love you," she said, caressing the brown hair at

the back of his neck.

"I love you," he said back, a soft light in his eyes. "Both of you."

She laid her head on his shoulder and happily swayed. When the dance ended, the DJ immediately launched into "Dancing Queen" by ABBA.

"Dammit, Jill," he muttered. "You promised no tricks."

Pressing away, she let her body start to move. "I couldn't resist. I am Mrs. Dancing Queen after all. Come on. You know how to move to this."

His groan was audible, but he started to dance nonetheless. Sure his movements were a bit awkward, and she found it endearing how his ears turned red as everyone joined them. But once they were surrounded by their family and friends, Brian settled down and got into his groove.

"You do know I'm praying our kid gets my dance moves," she told him as they wove to a Michael Bublé favorite.

"Trust me. I am too… We're so lucky, Jill."

She kissed him on the mouth and had to stop herself from taking the kiss further. "We are."

The dancing continued. At one point, they cut the coffee-and-cream wedding cake, and Jill didn't even mind when he spread a little of the cake across her lips. The espresso mousse and coffee-infused cake were a ridiculous combination.

When it came time to throw the bouquet, all the single women clustered in the center of the dance floor. She turned her back to the crowd and heaved the bouquet back with all her might. When she turned around, she saw Peggy shoving the bouquet at her cousin, Natalie, who was laughing uproariously with her sisters, Caroline and Moira.

"Guess she didn't want the bouquet," Mac said to Brian, giving Jill a wink.

She blew her new boss a kiss. Working with him at her new job was going to be so much fun.

They danced some more. Sometimes, she mingled with her cousins. Once, she managed to talk Uncle Arthur into dancing with her to an old Dean Martin classic.

By the end of the night, her feet hurt from dancing and her face hurt from smiling, but she was happier than she could ever remember being. When Brian slid his hands around her waist, she could feel something different in his touch.

"Are you ready to leave?" he asked her.

She looked up into his slumberous eyes. "Yep. Think we can get out of here?"

"If we have any trouble, I have an escape route planned through the kitchen."

Now that made her laugh, mostly because he looked completely serious.

They said goodbye to her family and made their way out of the hall. They'd agreed they didn't want to do a send-off or anything.

They drove to Aspen as the mountains slept in darkness. Their parents' friends had offered them the use of their cabin so they could have a proper honeymoon. With Brian starting up his restaurant, her starting her new job, and them buying a house, they'd agreed to do something less expensive for now. All that mattered was that they were together.

When they pulled into the circular driveway of the cabin, Brian came around to her door. She was barely out of the car before he swept her off her feet and pretended she was too heavy to carry.

"You do know the baby is like the size of a gum ball," she said in a playful huff.

"Must be all that cake you ate," he responded with a twinkle in his eyes.

She tapped him on the back of the head for that, but

somehow they managed to get inside the rustic cabin and find the light switches.

The entryway was covered in yellow rose petals, which extended up the hardwood stairs. Her heart squeezed.

"You did this?" she asked.

"I slipped away at daybreak," he told her, taking her hand and caressing her wedding ring. "I wanted tonight to be special for you."

She met his eyes. "It *is* special. You're here."

"Then let me light the candles and help you out of your dress," he said in a husky tone.

"Throw in a foot massage, and I'm there."

He laughed. "You've got it."

She must have nodded off during the foot massage because she awoke to find yellow ribbons of sunlight shining in her eyes. Brian was passed out next to her, snoring softly.

She rubbed her eyes. God, how pathetic. She'd fallen asleep on her own wedding night. Well, she'd heard it happened more often than not.

As the sun rose on the first day of her life as Brian McConnell's wife, she experienced the joy of waking up her new husband.

And he, in turn, showed her they would have many more lovely days of passion and fun and companionship.

He was, after all, her best friend *and* her husband now.

PEGGY & MAC

Peggy McBride had never liked weddings. All the attention and the fuss was like getting a tooth pulled in her opinion. Her first wedding had been a simple errand to the courthouse with her intended, another no-nonsense police officer like her. Sure she'd worn a dress, but that had been about as much tradition as she'd allowed.

Her second wedding—and she still couldn't believe she was saying that—was going to be at The Grand Mountain Hotel, owned by her fiancée, Mac Maven, a hotel mogul and a World Series of Poker champion. Mac was as smooth and charming as she was prickly. He dressed in tailored suits while she favored her green cotton deputy sheriff uniform. He liked bourbon while she usually chose beer.

On paper, they didn't seem to fit, but he was the love of her life. Go figure.

He'd known her well enough not to suggest a big wedding. She'd jokingly suggested getting hitched in Vegas, to which he'd only raised one of his elegant dark brows. No, Mac was going to have a stylish wedding, surrounded by their small group of friends and family in

Dare Valley.

Right now, she was pretty happy about the surrounded by friends and family part, if only because the presence of the Hale sisters was serving as a welcome distraction. She was trembling with nerves in her one-inch-heel wedding shoes, which actually had glitter on them. *Glitter.* How had she let Jill Hale talk her into that?

"Jill," she told her friend, who was sitting in a white suede chair in the penthouse Mac had reserved for her use as a dressing room. "I'm still not sure these shoes are me. Why can't I wear my plain old flats again?" Surely, it wasn't too late to make a switch.

Jill set her glass of champagne down and exchanged a look with her sister, Meredith, who was also Peggy's sister-in-law, preparing to tag-team her. She knew their strategy.

"Peggy," Jill said in an aggrieved tone. "The ceremony will be starting soon. It's too late to make a shoe change."

"Besides," Meredith added from her seat next to Jill on the couch, "the shoes add a little sparkle to your wedding ensemble since your dress is so classic."

Classic. Another word for *bo-ring.* She knew how they felt about her choice.

Since she barely ever wore dresses, wedding dress shopping had been one of the most painful experiences of her life—even worse than going lingerie shopping with the Hale sisters in Denver one time. They'd had her try on ten wedding dresses in three different styles until she'd put a stop to that nonsense and selected the simplest of the lot.

She'd chosen a high-neck, sleeveless number that fell in a straight line to the floor. The fabric cinched in under her breasts, but there wasn't an empire waist, thank God. The last thing she wanted to look like was a character in a Jane Austen novel. She'd refused to wear any adornments in her short page-boy styled hair. While shopping, she'd seen crowns that had horrified her and flower wreaths she'd feared would attract birds.

She hoped it could compete with Mac's selection of the most fabulously sexy tuxedo on the planet. She was quoting Jill here. The pattern on his jacket looked like chainmail, which made Peggy think of battle-scarred knights with broad-tipped swords. It was a perfectly tailored single-button jacket with a black satin notch lapel, according to Mac. Although unconventional in color and pattern, his tux exuded a classic style with its bow tie and pocket square, both in a color that reminded her of champagne, which matched the pattern on the jacket. The white shirt made everything pop, to her eye. It couldn't be classier. It couldn't be more him.

He'd joked that it would be bad luck for her to see his wedding day apparel before the ceremony. She hadn't been amused, so he'd finally caved. When she offered to show him what she planned to wear, he'd playfully gasped and clutched his heart like she'd committed the biggest wedding faux pas on the planet. Like she cared about stuff like that.

"You hate my dress," she said with a scowl.

"No," Jill immediately said, rushing off the couch. "It's simple and beautiful."

Yeah, that worked for her, although she wasn't sure about the beautiful part. She wasn't expecting anyone to say she was a beautiful bride. Even if they did, it would embarrass the hell out of her. She just didn't go for beauty.

"Ah...Mac has something he wanted us to give you," Meredith said, reaching into her purse.

When she pulled out an elegantly wrapped maroon package tied with a cream ribbon, Peggy experienced a brief moment of panic.

"Was I supposed to get him something too? Why didn't anyone tell me that?"

Weren't people supposed to give *them* gifts? Of course she thought that was weird too. Why did two people deserve a whole bunch of presents for getting sappy and falling in love?

"No, it's not mandatory," Meredith said, biting her lip to stop from grinning. "He just thought you might want to wear this."

Now she was suspicious. "What? Did he pick out my underwear or something? You might have mentioned that before I put this contraption on."

Jill barked out a laugh. "Pick out your underwear? That's a good one. I never thought about consulting with Brian on my undies before our wedding."

Peggy took the present and tore the paper off. Her hands started to sweat when she saw the black jewelry box, and then her mouth pretty much dropped to the earth's interior when she opened it. Inside was a necklace with the biggest red gem she'd ever seen. Two inches long, it looked like one of those stalagmites her son had done a book report on, except it was a brilliant, clear blood red.

"What is...it?" she asked a bit breathlessly. My God, it must have cost a fortune!

"It's a ruby, I believe," Meredith said, handing her a card. "I think he probably tells you that in here."

"Wowza," Jill said, gaping like a fish. "Now that's a rock."

A rock. Why would he give her a rock like this to wear? She was a deputy sheriff for heaven's sake. She caught the criminals who stole things like this. She opened the card.

Dear Peggy,
I know what you're thinking. Why in the hell did Mac give me something like this? Well, you need to understand the lore around rubies. I came across a passage about Burmese warriors wearing them to

*make themselves feel invincible in battle. I couldn't
think of a better talisman for the woman I'm marrying,
the warrior for justice who always puts herself in
harm's way to uphold law and order. I wanted you to
wear this today so you'd know—if you don't already—
that I love you as you are and will never try to change
you. So, my warrior bride, indulge me and wear this
today and every day you strap your gun to your side,
knowing it's my way of protecting you, even though I
know you can take care of yourself.*

All my love,
Mac

A huge ball of emotion rose in her chest as she
gripped the note. Crap. That man always knew how to
get to her. His warrior bride. She rather liked the sound
of that. When she set the card aside and pulled the
necklace out of the box, her palms weren't sweating
anymore. The gold chain was long enough for her to pull
it over her head. The gem fell just past her breasts,
which was good since Mac knew she didn't like drawing
attention to them.

"It's beautiful," Meredith said with an audible sigh.

"Can I read the note?" Jill asked, as eager as a nosy
neighbor.

"Sure, why not? At least someone will know why I'm
wearing it. Anyone else will think it looks ridiculous on
me."

Meredith tunneled in closer to her sister to read the
note, and soon there were alarming tears popping into
their eyes.

"That man is the single most romantic man on the
planet," Jill said wistfully. "Burmese warriors. He's a
Renaissance man, that's for sure. Which is why I love
working for him."

"He's a keeper," Meredith agreed, "and he's right. It
does suit you. Peggy, the warrior bride."

And as she turned to look in the mirror on the wall, she saw herself in a new light. She looked powerful, like Joan of Arc must have looked as she led men into battle. Perhaps Mac did know her better than she knew herself.

***

Of all the ways Mac had expected to pass the time before his wedding in the private suite he'd commandeered, it hadn't been singing. No, he'd thought he and his friends might play poker. Smoke a few cigars. Well, they'd smoked a few cigars with their bourbon, but no one had mentioned cards, much to his surprise.

No, his dear old friend, Rhett Butler Blaylock, had talked their mutual friend, country singer Rye Crenshaw, into leading a rendition of "God Bless The Broken Road." A man of romantic notions, Rhett claimed it reminded him of Mac and Peggy.

Most of the guys joined in as soon as Rye started strumming out the song on his red guitar, and the sing-along had continued from there. Rhett couldn't carry a tune if his life depended on it, and so far it hadn't, or he'd be dead. Fortunately, Mac's other friends *could* carry a tune, so between Rye and Clayton Chandler and John Parker McGuiness, Rhett's mulish braying could hardly be heard.

"Those things stink," Keith, his soon-to-be son, said. The boy stood at his side, pointing at his cigar with distaste.

The cigar's acrid scent offended some people, but to Mac, the one he was enjoying smelled like tea, tobacco, and cardamom. He could almost imagine other poker players in times past smoking them in Macau when the Portuguese influence there was strong.

"Cigars are like bourbon," he told Keith. "You either like them or you don't. And it'll be years before you're old enough to find out which it is for you."

Mac paused to listen to Rye's rendition of the old Tim McGraw classic, "My Next Thirty Years," which he thought was fitting for his wedding day. He had no trouble imagining himself and Peggy and Keith thirty years from now. She'd still be kicking criminal butt, and he'd still be playing poker and running hotels.

With any luck, their family would be bigger than it was now. Peggy was open to having more kids, and he was more than excited about that. Helping his single-mom sister raise his nephew, Dustin, who was currently arm-in-arm with Rhett, singing right along with the rest of the guys, had shown him how much he wanted to be a father. And Keith, whom he already loved as a son, had shown him what a wonderful mother Peggy was. After growing up in a dysfunctional household, he couldn't wait to have the family he'd always dreamed about.

"Why don't I open a window?" Mac said to the boy, who was now pinching his nose with his thumb and forefinger.

Even though it was winter, a slight breeze would help. Besides, the last thing he wanted was for Peggy's nose to wrinkle up at the cigar scent when she met him at the end of the aisle.

"Mom won't let you smoke those in our house," Keith informed him with a serious frown.

"I know she won't, so when I have a hankering for one, I'll have one here," Mac said as he opened the nearest window. "Okay?"

He thought for a moment and then gave him a serious nod. "Okay. Maybe I can try them one day when I get older since you like them so much. But we can't tell mom. She wouldn't like it." He often acted a lot older than his seven years, and Mac knew it came from being raised by a single mom.

"No, she wouldn't like it." On that they could agree.

"And I have to be eighteen to smoke. It's the law."

He had to bite his lip to keep from smiling. Keith

knew every age limit associated with every law for the average citizen, courtesy of his law-enforcing mother. "You'll be at least eighteen. I promise."

"Good," he said, wrinkling his nose again. "Can I have another soda?"

"How many have you had?" The country music spectacle had distracted him enough that he'd lost count.

Keith looked over his shoulder. "Hey, Dustin! How many sodas have I had?"

His nephew kept on singing, swaying with Rhett now, but he held up two fingers.

"Two?" Mac said. "How about some water? Your mom doesn't like you to drink soda."

The boy kicked out his right foot like he was kicking an invisible rock. "I know. She says it's bad for my teeth and makes me jittery."

"Maybe you can have another after the ceremony," Mac said in an easy tone. "Today is a pretty special day."

"It sure is," the boy said with a bright smile now, showing a missing tooth. "You're going to be my real dad. In the eyes of the law and everything."

He pulled the boy in for a hug. "And everything. Now go on over to the bar, and grab a water."

"Okay," Keith said and darted off after squeezing him tight.

Mac sat back on the leather couch and surveyed the snow falling in the mountains outside. Somehow it only added romance to the scene. Then he shook his head. He was pretty much seeing romance in just about everything today. He wondered if Peggy felt the same way—even though she wasn't particularly sentimental. How would she react to his wedding present? Her first response would probably be anxiety over the expense. His money still made her nervous. Then she would panic about wearing it. But hopefully she would soften once she read the note. Well, he would find out as soon as he saw her at the ceremony.

"Mac Maverick Maven," Rhett called out. "Come on over here and sing with us. We need another bass."

They didn't, but he rose from the couch and spared a glance for his future brother-in-law, who sat in an arm chair with a bourbon in his hand.

"Are you planning to join us?" he asked Tanner. "I don't think I can fight Rhett off any longer."

"Sorry," he said with a shake of his head. "You have to face the lions alone. Or throw them out."

Even though he knew the man was teasing, he stroked his chin as if considering the suggestion. "If Rhett's voice brings in the hounds, we might have to."

Since he wouldn't put it past Rhett to corral Dustin into dragging him over if he didn't come willingly, Mac strolled over to join the singing party. Some of the guys were casually sitting on bar stools while others were standing. Rhett had joked that his location was closer to the Pappy Van Winkle, but the man hadn't touched his bourbon for over an hour. He'd been too busy singing like a lark.

"Mac, my boy," Rhett said, reeling him in with a meaty hand. "Good of you to join us."

Mac took his position on Rhett's right side while Dustin peered at him from the man's left.

"Hiya, Uncle Mac," he said, grinning in that dopey, delighted way teenage boys did when they were included in adult male rituals.

"Hi, Dustin," he said and gave his nephew a high five.

Rhett jostled them both when he wrapped his arms around their shoulders.

"Do you have a request, Mac?" Rye said, fingering the chords.

He gave them all a sly smile. "How about 'I Have Friends In Low Places?'"

Rhett slapped him on the back. "Now, I know you—

mean that to be a joke, but I do love that song. Rye?"

The country singer's only response was to start playing, and that was how Mac Maven ended up singing a Garth Brooks classic on his wedding day.

***

Jill was acting like a rabid beauty queen in her attempts to strong-arm Peggy into putting on a darker lip gloss. She'd balked at lipstick since she rarely—read almost never—wore makeup. But Jill was sneaky. She'd convinced Peggy to let her dab some powder and a splash of color onto her cheeks so she could avoid grease shine in her wedding photos, which was when she had stealthily swiped the first round of lip gloss onto her mouth. Since it hadn't looked terrible, Peggy had kept it on.

"Jill, I am not going to put Plum Berry or whatever that is on my lips," she said, crossing her arms. Who came up with names like that, anyway? "I have more than enough goo on my face."

"But it will match your ruby," Jill protested. "We have to change your lip gloss."

Match her ruby? "Because of my necklace? What planet are you from?"

"Venus," Meredith said, and when Peggy gave her a blank look, she added, "Never mind. Jill, leave the poor bride alone."

Jill re-inserted the wand into the container, and Peggy breathed a sigh of relief.

The door to the suite clicked open and inside ran her son, followed by her brother, Tanner.

"Mom!" Keith said, coming to a stop in front of her. "You've got to see what Dad set up in the reception area. It's so cool. It's a S'mores bar with a fire and everything. He said he did it for me. Isn't that the coolest? Of course, he said I'd need to share because other people like S'mores too."

Her heart melted like a glob of wax under a flame. Keith had already taken to calling Mac "Dad" because he adored him. Thank God the feeling was mutual since Keith's father pretty much defined deadbeat. Who else but Mac would have thought about giving her son something special on their wedding day?

"That sounds pretty cool," she said. Her son's tiny bow tie was slightly crooked, which only made it more adorable.

"Wow!" Keith said. "Where did you get that?"

He was pointing to her necklace, his eyes as wide as saucers.

"Your...dad gave it to me." She was still practicing calling him that. Each time she said it, she felt a funny pinch in her heart.

"Cool!" he said and then ran over to give Jill and Meredith hugs.

Tanner halted the moment he saw her. "Wow. Peggy you look incredible. Who's responsible for the lip stuff?"

He knew her too well.

Jill raised her hand. "Me! Isn't it great?"

"*Fabulous*," he drolled and strolled over to kiss his wife as soon as Keith let her go. "How are you ladies faring?"

"We're good," Meredith told him. "How is the groom's party doing?"

Peggy hadn't wanted to fret with attendants or anything. The idea of having bridesmaids walk down the aisle in gowns she'd selected was more abhorrent to her than a prison sentence. Still, she couldn't deny she was grateful to have Meredith and Jill with her now.

"Rhett talked Rye into singing," Tanner told them, "so they've been belting out country classics for all of an hour. Mac even joined in on 'I've Got Friends in Low Places.'"

"Shut the front door," Peggy said. "I've never heard

him sing." Okay, maybe a couple times in the shower, but she so wasn't sharing that.

"Yeah, it was so cool, Mom," Keith said. "Rhett is so off-key he's breaking everyone's eardrums, but everyone else is really good."

Tanner ruffled his hair. "That's what Rye said."

"Yeah," Keith said in that eager high-pitched voice of his. "And Rye is the best guitar player ever. He even taught me some chords."

"That was nice of him," Peggy commented. Rye and Rhett were two flavors of the same kind of trouble, all right, but somehow they always ended up making her smile. That didn't mean she didn't watch them like a hawk though.

"I was told to come and get you," Tanner said. "We're getting close to wedding time. Keith, come here and let me straighten your bow tie."

Her son squirmed under her brother's ministrations, as eager as a kid who'd just downed a whole bag of Halloween candy.

"Okay, Mom," he said when he finally darted away from his uncle. "Let's go get married."

To Keith's mind, they were both marrying Mac, and she had thought it was too cute to correct him. Besides, in some ways, Mac *was* marrying them both. And that's why she was having Keith walk down the aisle with her. She was too old to have anyone give her away, and that tradition seemed kind of weird to her anyway. Not that she had a father to give her away.

They all left the penthouse and took the elevator down to the main floor where they would have the wedding.

Waiting for them in the lobby was Mac's assistant, who was handling most of the wedding arrangements. She looked relieved to see them. "Wonderful. You're here. Let me go grab your bouquet. Head on down the hall to the event room, and I'll meet you there."

She nodded and led their group *to the event room*, which sounded way too official to Peggy's ears. Simply put, it was a fancy room the hotel used for gatherings. And the location was one of a handful of decisions Peggy had been loath to make.

Fortunately, the whole flower thing had been taken off her plate. Mac's sister, Abbie, had made her bouquet personally, and not just because she handled all the flower arrangements at Mac's hotel. She'd designed it with Mac's input because Peggy had grown clammy at the mere mention of wedding colors—another wedding horror to her mind. Why they needed to pick colors she still didn't understand, but Mac had chosen white and blush. It turned out that blush was the kind of soft pink people painted a nursery for a baby girl. Peggy was surprised by how much she didn't dislike it. Pink was so not her thing.

The woman returned moments later with a bouquet of white and blush-colored roses with a pink sprig of something too lacy and delicate to survive the hour. The ribbon-wrapped stems felt awkward in Peggy's hands, and she was afraid she'd break them without trying.

While she might have delegated the wedding flower and color choices to Mac and Abbie, she had drawn the line in the sand on one thing. Peggy wasn't really a bouquet thrower, so there would be none of that single ladies nonsense. It was too embarrassing.

Having delivered the bouquet, Mac's helper was now pinning a boutonniere on Keith, who was squirming again. She couldn't blame him.

Tanner put his hand on her arm and gave her a soft smile, like he knew the thought of everyone staring at her as she walked down the aisle was making her get all fidgety. "Break a leg."

She laughed half-heartedly, and then Jill and Meredith hugged her and disappeared behind the massively carved wooden double doors.

The woman checked her watch—a fanciful confection with diamonds around the face. Peggy couldn't imagine wearing a watch like that, but then again who was she to judge? She was wearing a giant ruby around her neck.

"Two minutes and counting," the woman said in a drill-sergeant tone.

Did she plan on counting down the seconds when they got to ten like it was New Year's Eve? Peggy hoped not.

Keith curled his hand in hers, and she looked down at him. His brow was furrowed.

"Are you nervous?" she asked, wishing her stomach would stop acting like there were magic jumping beans inside it.

"No," he said quietly. "I just...don't want to mess anything up."

She dropped to her haunches so they were eye level. "You could never do that."

"That's what Dad said," he muttered, looking down at his shiny black shoes.

"Well, he's right," she told him, smoothing down his cowlick. "This is our special day, and *nothing* could ruin it."

"Because we're really going to be a family now, right? In the eyes of the law and everything?"

Her heart swelled with pride. "Yes, in the eyes of the law and everything."

"Then it's going to be okay. Dad says us being a family is all that matters."

She couldn't agree more. She knew she and Mac were going to last. She knew it like she knew she wanted to be a cop.

She stood, and all her nerves about being in the spotlight slipped away. The woman opened the doors, and suddenly a long aisle with a white runner stretched out in front of her. She took a step, feeling Keith match her stride.

Together, they walked down the aisle.

***

Mac had thought Peggy's brother would give her away. And since Peggy had balked at a wedding rehearsal, saying, "How hard can it be to walk a straight line?" he hadn't pressed.

But he hadn't been prepared. Not for this.

The woman who'd captured his heart was walking toward him hand-in-hand with the little boy he already thought of as his son. And she was wearing the ruby pendant he'd given her. As far as life moments went, this one was pure perfection, and he almost wished she'd walk slower so he could savor it. But even with "Here Comes The Bride" being played by the orchestra he'd hired, she couldn't stop herself from giving into her natural gait: a power walk.

Keith was grinning, and as soon as he cleared the last row of chairs decorated with roses in white and blush, he let go of his mom's hand and ran to Mac.

"Dad!" he cried as Mac swept him up into his arms. "We're getting married. Finally!"

"Amen," Rhett added from the front row.

The guests all laughed, and Mac felt a grin tug at his mouth.

"I'm glad you brought your mom down the aisle," he told Keith. "That was a nice surprise."

"Mom said we both had to do it since you'll be living with both of us now," Keith said, his missing tooth utterly charming as he smiled back at Mac.

He was moving into her smaller house with them because she wasn't comfortable with the thought of something grander yet. Honestly, he didn't mind where they lived as long as they were there together.

His gaze shifted to Peggy, who seemed a bit out of

her element, like she had no idea what to do with the bouquet in her hand. He gave his assistant a significant look, and as perceptive as always, she stepped forward and took the flowers before disappearing into the background.

"Give me a big hug, and then go sit by your Uncle Tanner," Mac told Keith, squeezing him tight. "I need to say hi to your mom."

Peggy was watching them patiently with a small smile, giving them their moment together.

As soon as he set the boy down, Keith ran over to Peggy and wrapped his arms around her. "Go get married, Mom." Then he ran to the open chair next to his uncle.

"I'll be a good father to him," he told her quietly.

"I know," she simply responded.

Mac covered the short distance between them, grabbed Peggy's hand, and raised it to his lips for a kiss—simply to fluster her. "You look beautiful."

"You look...like you." Then she gave a charming blush. "I mean...you look handsome—like usual."

The grin he'd been fighting broke free. She was still working on mastering compliments—the giving and the accepting of them. "The pendant suits you, my Warrior Bride," he said, wanting to caress her cheek but refraining. There would be plenty of time for that later, once the guests departed.

"If you hadn't come up with that story, I don't think I could have worn it," she said in that purely honest way of hers, fingering the ruby.

"I know," he said because he admired the way she always told the truth. He led her to where the minister stood. "Let's make this legal."

Her mouth tipped up at his use of her vernacular, and for the rest of the ceremony, everything faded until the moment she said her vows to him and accepted his ring on her finger.

There was that special light in her brown eyes, the one reserved only for him, as he said his vows to her, and his chest swelled from all the love in his heart.

When the minister pronounced them husband and wife and said he could kiss the bride, Peggy stayed in his arms longer than he'd expected. Her mouth softened, and she even gave one of her breathless sighs. The kind that shattered his control.

He forced himself to step away from her and tucked her arm through his own. Then he leaned down and said, "I love you. Never forget that."

She turned her head up to him. "I won't."

"Good," he responded and held out his hand to Keith, who came bounding over to take it.

Together, the three of them walked down the aisle as a family.

***

Receptions were a funny thing, Peggy decided as she excused herself to find the ladies' room. They hadn't invited a lot of people, but it had felt awkward greeting everyone in the reception line, particularly since so many of the guests had pulled her into hugs without even asking. Mac had been his usual smooth self, thanking people for coming, graciously accepting their congratulations. She'd mostly been tongue-tied. Halfway through, Mac had leaned over and whispered in her ear, "Don't worry. It's almost over."

Of course, she didn't mind talking to the people she knew, but it was weird having people stand in line for the privilege.

As she was turning around to head to the ladies' room, Rhett swept her off her feet and swung her around, making her seriously consider whacking that crazy Southern loon in the back of the head. But even she knew it would be frowned upon for the bride to smack a guest. She was a police officer, after all. Of course if the guest were being fresh, she wouldn't hesitate for a second. She'd smack him with just cause and then some.

"You look beautiful," Rhett said, setting her back on her feet. "And you just made my buddy the happiest man on earth."

She'd thought no one but Mac, who liked to say crazy things to her, would call her beautiful, but there had been dozens of compliments. "Ah...thanks. I...ah...need to go to the bathroom." Jeez, could this be any more awkward?

Rhett playfully tapped her on the shoulder. "Don't take too long in the powder room, or Mac will be wasting away from missing you."

The powder room? Wasting away? She gave him a wan smile and boogied away from his brand of craziness to the bathroom. As she was washing her hands under the luxurious gold sink—who had a gold sink?—Jill bounded into the bathroom.

"How about some more lip gloss?" she asked, opening her clutch.

"How about you find someone else for Makeup Torture Hour?" she bandied back.

"Come on," Jill pleaded. "Brian is taking care of the twins with my mom and dad right now. This is probably my only adult moment for the rest of the night."

Even though she knew Jill was stretching the truth, she caved. "Okay. But only lip gloss."

Jill rushed over, her glistening wand already in hand. "Are you sure? Because I swear, your eyes would seriously pop with a little mascara."

They had already argued about this, and she'd won that round. "You *will* die if you so much as make a move toward my eyes," she said without a trace of humor in her voice.

"Would you leave my twin girls motherless?" Jill

asked with crocodile tears popping into her eyes. Never underestimate Jill.

"Yes," she said since she knew they were joking. "Now, swipe that crap on my lips and go to the can. Isn't that why you came in here?"

"No," her friend said, touching the lip gloss to her mouth like Peggy was a model in New York's fashion week. "I came in here for this."

"You are so weird."

"I know," she replied with a lopsided grin. "We're a match made in heaven."

When she left the bathroom with Jill, Rhett caught her again before she could make it to the head table. The man seemed to have her in his sights today, and she couldn't understand why.

"All right now," he drawled, giving her outfit an eyeful. "Instead of wearing a garter, did you strap your gun to your thigh?"

She'd considered it for a moment, but she knew Mac wouldn't have approved. He had his own security for the hotel, but you never could tell what might happen. She liked to be prepared. She felt almost naked without her gun—not that she was going to say that to Rhett. He'd only start talking nonsense about getting *buck* naked, one of his favorite topics. She still didn't understand what a "buck" had to do with it. And she wasn't going to ask.

"I'm not carrying," she replied, trying to move past him.

He waggled his brows. "You're a woman of mystery. Thanks for marrying my friend. He's pretty besotted with you."

Besotted? Would his platitudes never end? "Thanks. I guess." Her cheeks were flushing with embarrassment now.

He extended his arm like the gentleman he wasn't. "May I show you to your chair, my lady?"

What was this? Knights of the Round Table? "I can manage. It's like twenty feet away, Rhett."

Ignoring her, he grabbed her arm. "A lady doesn't say no to a gentleman."

"You're no gentleman," she responded, watching as Keith bounced up and down in his chair at the head table.

She met Mac's stoplight-green eyes as she neared the table, and her insides dissolved like the tissue paper stuffed into the wedding present bags up front.

"No, ma'am, I'm not, but then again you had my number the minute you laid eyes on me." Rhett pulled out her chair and winked at her before taking his seat next to Mac's nephew, Dustin, who was between Mac and his mother, Abbie.

Rhett cast Abbie a look of pure longing and then turned to speak with Rye. They were getting along better, Peggy knew, but Abbie still hadn't relented to his continued pursuit. The man was a proverbial sap. It was kinda sweet when he wasn't being crazy.

"I see Rhett is giving you his unique brand of attention," Mac whispered and kissed her cheek. "He's happy to see me settled. You should have heard the country songs he dedicated to our marriage before the ceremony started."

"I heard about that." She fingered the chainmail sleeve of his jacket and bit her lip. "I even heard you ended up singing Garth Brooks."

He gave her a look. "That is never to be repeated."

"I can keep your secrets," she said, wishing they didn't have all these people around them so she could do something sappy and kiss him until they were both senseless.

"I know you can," he said, laying his hand over hers on his sleeve. "Later."

She felt that one word all the way to her toes. It took some effort to look away from him and remove her hand, but she managed. The water cooled her hot throat.

Shaking herself, she made herself look past her delectable groom. "Abbie, thanks again for all your help," she told her new sister-in-law. "Everything looks beautiful."

While Mac had plenty of minions to see to his instructions, Abbie had insisted on personally seeing to many of the last-minute preparations for the wedding, which was why she hadn't joined Peggy, Jill, and Meredith in the penthouse.

"You're most welcome," Abbie said, holding her champagne glass in that elegant way of hers. "You know how much I love planning parties. I think everyone's going to enjoy themselves, don't you?"

Was Peggy responsible for ensuring they were having a good time? She clutched the wine glass Mac handed her. "I'm sure it will be all right."

"Breathe," Mac said in a whisper. "You don't have anything more pressing to do than eat, dance with me, and cut the cake."

"We have to cut the cake?" she asked. She hadn't thought to put a stop to that. It was more of that spotlight stuff she hated.

"It's a simple tradition. Don't pretend you've never heard of it."

"I was hoping some of your people would do it. Your hotel has knives, right?"

He leaned in until she could feel his hot breath on her ear. "Stop toying with me. I'll only make you pay later."

She gave a quick glance to make sure her son wasn't listening, but he was talking to Tanner, who was sitting next to him. "Promise?"

"Have I ever let you down?" he asked.

"No," she said.

When she lifted her glass to her mouth, she tasted

beer, which she liked a heck of a lot better than wine. No, he had never let her down.

The servers came around with their food. Mac had wanted a sit-down meal for the reception, and she'd chosen surf and turf. There would be no rubber chicken dinner for her on her wedding day.

The lobster tail was bathed in enough butter to sink a ship, and the prime rib had just enough blood to remind her of her ruby. She shook her head. That man was making her crazy. Now she was comparing beef juice and jewels. Someone should call Robin Leach so he could bring *Lifestyles of the Rich and Famous* back to primetime.

The band Mac had selected was playing some classy instrumental that reminded her of the Rat Pack. Pretty soon, she'd have to dance with him—just the two of them—on the parquet dance floor in the center of the room. He'd insisted they have a dance. Her heart rate kicked up at the very thought. She sucked at dancing, which she'd tried to tell him, and she was bound to step on his toes.

Throughout the meal Keith continued to run back and forth to visit with all his favorite people, and she didn't have the heart to tell him to stay in one place. Not after the way he'd shoveled down his meal as fast as possible so he could be excused from the table. Right now, he was talking with his adopted grandfather, Arthur Hale, and she pushed her chair back to say hello to him. They'd only had a perfunctory hug earlier in the reception line.

"And where are you going, my dear?" Mac asked, taking her hand.

"I'd like to talk to Arthur," she told him. "I'm finished eating."

She was going to wish for her fat pants by the time they got to the cake. But how could she not look forward to all that sugar? Selecting a wedding cake had been her favorite part of wedding planning. Who *didn't* like trying ten types of cake and selecting the best of the lot?

Mac had ceded to her tastes there, and she'd chosen a dark chocolate cake with raspberry filling and white buttercream frosting. The cake lady had wanted to put white frosting roses on the cake to make it pretty, and while Peggy had thought it too fussy, she'd agreed after seeing some of the more insanely complicated cake decorations.

"How about I join you?" Mac asked, rising from his chair. "We can make the rounds."

"The rounds?" She almost gulped.

"Yes. You know. Talk to our guests at each of their tables."

All of the sudden she wanted to sit back down. "We have to talk to them more?"

"Don't sound so horrified," he said, and she could hear the repressed laughter in his voice. "Now, smile."

She pasted on a smile, but when she caught sight of Arthur handing Keith one of his signature red hot candies, she didn't have to fake anything.

"I could use one of those too," she said to the older man when they reached them.

He tossed her one with a wink. She caught it deftly in her hand.

"Thanks, Arthur."

"My bride gave me red hots on my wedding day," he told her, and she was alarmed to see him grow misty-eyed. Arthur Hale wrote about war and climate change. He was not supposed to tear up while talking about red hots.

"No wonder you keep them around," Mac said and surprised her by taking one of the candies Arthur held out to him. "They must bring back wonderful memories of your beloved Harriet."

The older man coughed to clear his voice. "Harriet would have liked you, Peggy, as I've told you before. She was tough like you. But inside she was as soft as cream cheese."

"Mom hates cream cheese," Keith said. "She doesn't even like cheesecake. Isn't that the weirdest thing ever?"

"The weirdest," Arthur replied seriously, crunching on his red hot. "You make a lovely bride, my dear. It's nice to see a woman dress up without all that froufrou."

Jill rolled her eyes from her seat beside him. "You'd better not be talking about me, Grandpa. I won't let you hold Mia anymore tonight."

He reached for his granddaughter's cooing baby. "Then I am most definitely not talking about you, Jillie Bean."

After chatting with the Hales for a few minutes, Peggy and Mac moved on to the next table. At Mac's suggestion, they'd invited Peggy's fellow police officers, so they joined them and their wives and made small talk and joked about having a tower of donuts instead of a wedding cake and other silly things. Thank God no one commented about her necklace, but she'd seen a few of the guys eye it—and her—like she'd gone mad. When she returned from her honeymoon in San Francisco, she expected them to tease her about it. She'd have to plan a reply that would shut down that line of joking.

By the time she and Mac walked away from the last table, her shoulders weren't stiff and tense anymore. Talking to people wasn't *that* bad, although it was weird for everyone else to be sitting down while she and Mac were standing. Then she heard the band cue up the song Mac had picked for them, and her shoulders went back to being ramrod straight.

"Do we really have to dance?" she asked. "Please, don't make me." It embarrassed her to beg, but she suddenly felt overwhelmed. She'd been on display so much today.

"Yes, we do, but I have an idea that might make it easier on you." He gave a soft whistle by putting his two fingers to that gorgeous mouth of his. Keith came running.

"Is it time to dance?" her son asked.

His mini-tuxedo jacket—courtesy of Mac—had come unbuttoned. His shirt was partially tucked in. And sure enough, his bow tie was crooked again. He looked absolutely adorable.

"Yep," Mac said, taking her hand and Keith's and leading them onto the dance floor.

The music flowed through the room, and as she stood there holding the hands of her favorite men, Peggy decided she could be silly for just once in her life and dance. She got jiggy to the beat.

***

It was a rarity to see Peggy bust out her moves, and Mac didn't intend to squander the occasion. He sent Keith off to dance with Abbie when the first song ended. Just as he'd expected, Peggy made a move to leave the dance floor, but he snaked a hand around her waist.

"Not just yet," he whispered into her ear.

Couples strolled onto the floor around them, and he swayed with her to the orchestra's medley.

"You tricked me," she accused with a narrowing of her gorgeous eyes.

"I thought you might loosen up a little if we shared our first dance with Keith, but I was still hoping we'd have a dance for just the two of us." He stepped back and led her into a twirl.

She looked at him like he'd gone as crazy as Rhett. Peggy McBride wasn't a woman who twirled.

"You do look beautiful," he said softly.

Her face flushed. "Thanks...this whole wedding stuff is...kinda nice. When it's not awkward."

To ease her discomfort, he brought her close and whispered in her ear, "How about we cut the cake soon?

That way, we can leave whenever you want." He was more than eager to leave for his own reasons.

"You mean we can leave with all these people here?" she asked, looking around the room like the idea had never dawned on her.

"It's our wedding," he told her. "We can do whatever we want."

"Why didn't you tell me we could do anything we wanted before today?" she asked with an edge of delightful suspicion to her voice.

"Because you would have insisted on getting married in Vegas, and I didn't think you truly wanted that."

Now her eyes had really narrowed. "You didn't?"

"No," he said, turning her in a half circle so they looked like they were doing at least some dancing and not just standing and chatting. "Under all of that bluster, you like to be around our new friends and family."

The corners of her mouth tipped up, and he knew he had her. Sometimes she was as full of bluster as Arthur Hale. Not that he would tell that to the older man or his new wife.

"You might be right," she said, "but don't test that premise by making me dance with Rhett. I think he's waiting in the wings for us to finish."

Mac looked over, and sure enough, his friend was standing on the edge of the dance floor next to Dustin. Rhett gave him a thumbs-up, which made him laugh.

"You'll be happy to know I instructed the orchestra not to accept any requests from Rhett."

"Thank God."

"Or Jill."

Now she gave him a full-blown smile. "Nothing gets past you, does it?"

Oh, how daring his Warrior Bride looked under the soft light of the chandeliers above them. "You didn't."

And as he spun her around in his arms, he knew she'd keep him on his toes for the next thirty years and then some, and he couldn't wait to see what their family would look like down that long, beautiful road.

Abbie & Rhett

Planning a wedding with a man as outlandish as Rhett Butler Blaylock had been a daring task for Abbie Maven. He loved and catered to her too much to leave all the details to her. But good heavens, they'd had to balance two very different visions of their big day.

Rhett wanted what he termed a rip-roaring Southern BBQ feast the likes of which Dare Valley had never seen. When Abbie had expressed her concern about eating an entrée with a dark red tomato sauce that could stain her wedding gown, Rhett had only laughed and said they'd wear specialty wedding bibs. *Bibs.* The man was insane.

But Mac's chef had promised her he could accommodate Rhett's BBQ extravaganza with her more conventional Americana menu by arranging a massive buffet guaranteed to stuff their guests to the gills. Rhett would have his dry-rub baby back ribs and crayfish boil with roasted corn and new potatoes while she would have her selections of roast chicken, prime rib, and sea bass.

The alcohol had required some compromise as well. Rhett had insisted on beer kegs—something Abbie had never imagined at a wedding—while she had arranged for her champagne fountain. And of course, he'd insisted on a selection of fine bourbons for their guests' enjoyment, and mint juleps for the more daring. Fortunately, Rhett's favorite spirit could easily be stocked at the bar along with her selections of pinot grigio and cabernet sauvignon.

He'd left the cake completely up to her. She would have her delicious three layer apricot-filled Lady Baltimore cake with buttercream frosting the color of the Sweet Juliet rose, her favorite flower. All Rhett had asked was that his groom's cake be chocolate and have something to do with poker. His face had looked oh-so eager as he showed her a picture of a two-tiered cake decorated with the card suits of hearts, diamonds, spades, and clubs, so she'd sighed and compromised.

She had a feeling marriage to Rhett would involve a lot of compromises, but since she loved him so darn much, she truly didn't mind. Except when his ideas were outright crazy.

Abbie stood in front of the mirror in her hotel suite and took one last look at her dress. She wasn't a young bride. Heavens, she had a teenage son. A big, flouncy wedding gown simply wouldn't do. But the simple, one-shoulder, cream-colored satin gown with a draped bodice reminiscent of old Hollywood was perfect. She loved the way it clung to her skin. Rhett would swallow his tongue when he saw her. Then she laughed at herself. She was already picking up some of his unusual Southernisms that she found so charming.

Someone knocked on the door, and she looked in the mirror one last time to make sure her French twist was secure. Not a curl was out of place. A smile spread across her face as she opened the door. The two men who had helped her become who she was today stood in the opening: her brother and her son.

"Wow, Mom," Dustin gushed, looking way too

grown up in the pale blue suit Rhett had chosen for his groomsmen. "You look hot. Rhett's mouth is going to dry up like an old well when he sees you."

Obviously she wasn't the only one who'd resorted to thinking in Rhett-isms. "Why thank you, Dustin. Although I don't know if it's appropriate to tell your mother she looks hot."

He flushed red. "Okay, you're right. It's weird."

Mac leaned in and bussed her cheek so as to not mess up her makeup. "Abbie, you look timeless. I don't think you've ever been more beautiful."

She pressed her lips together when she felt tears wet her lashes. "Oh, don't say such things. I'm going to cry."

"I thought all brides cried on their wedding day," he mused. "Even tough ones who carry firearms for work."

Peggy must have been hiding off to the side because she emerged in the opening with her son, Keith. "You do look nice, Abbie." She winced, as if hearing the understatement in her own words. "You know I'm no good with all this girl stuff."

"Yeah, Aunt Abbie, you look bea-u-ti-ful," Keith said in a dramatic tone. The seven-year-old, who took his duties as ring bearer with an appropriate solemnity, looked as cute as a button in a mini version of the suit ensemble her brother and Dustin were wearing.

Her new sister-in-law was more comfortable cuffing criminals than she was around weddings, which is why she hadn't suggested she help Abbie dress or do her hair and makeup. It would have been too...strange. In truth, she'd rather enjoyed doing it all alone—something she'd wanted to do since the few times she'd been made up by so-called experts, she had ended up not looking like herself. The time alone had been a rare quiet moment in the chaos leading up to the wedding.

"Come inside," she told her family and led them into the main salon of the suite.

Mac had given her the best one they had in The

Grand Mountain Hotel. Outside, it was snowing lightly, and the carpet of white gave Dare Valley a delightfully picturesque feel. She hadn't expected to marry in winter, but neither of them had wanted to wait, so they'd simply said poo to the cold weather and set the date. The location had been an obvious choice, particularly since Rhett's only other suggestion had been an Elvis chapel in Vegas...and he'd later admitted to "funnin' with her" by suggesting it.

"How about a drink?" she asked them.

"You don't have to serve us, Abbie," her brother said. "It's your big day. How about we have a family toast?"

"Me too?" Dustin said with more glee than she cared for.

Mac cocked an eyebrow in her direction. "Ask your mother."

"Half a glass," she said as Mac stepped behind the suite's bar to pick out a fabulous bottle of Dom Perignon she'd seen in the cooler.

The cork flew across the room when he popped it, and Peggy handed him four crystal flutes from one of the glossy mahogany cabinets. Then she poured sparking water into a glass and handed it to Keith.

"Someday, I'll be big enough to have champagne," Keith said wistfully.

"Yes, you will, but not today," his mother said. "You have to be twenty-one."

His brow furrowed. "But Dustin isn't twenty-one. Are you going to arrest him?"

Her son gulped, and Abbie almost laughed.

Peggy gave him a pointed glance. "I think Dustin and I understand each other. This is a special occasion, and he won't be driving."

"No, not driving or anything," he assured her with an emphatic nod. "In fact, I'm barely going to take a drink."

Like she believed that one. "Is the driveway to the hotel clear? You plowed all the new snow, right?" she asked Mac when he handed her a glass. The yeasty smell tickled her nose.

"Abbie," he said in that same indulgent tone he'd used with her all her life when she fretted. "I told you everything would be perfect."

And it would be. Mac knew how to make everything perfect.

"Okay, I'm just a little nervous."

"Chill, Mom," Dustin told her, raising the glass to take a swig.

Mac stopped him with a gentle hand. "We toast first, kid."

"Sorry."

Extending his glass to her, Mac simply said, "To my sister, Abbie, one of the best women in the world. I am so happy to see you marrying one of my closest friends. May you always be as radiant as you are today."

She dabbed at her eye with her free hand. "Oh, Mac."

He hugged her close, and they had a moment. For so long, they'd been partners both in business and in the raising of her son. Now all of that was changing. He was living with Peggy and Keith, and she and Dustin would be living with Rhett.

"Here now," he murmured and set his champagne glass aside untouched so he could fish out a monogrammed pink handkerchief that matched his silk tie and vest.

The handkerchief did the job, but she was afraid she'd have to touch up her makeup before they headed to the suite where she and Rhett would say their vows. After planning her wedding, she'd talked Mac into making one of their suites available for weddings since there weren't too many event spaces for such occasions beyond the churches in Dare Valley.

She finally took a sip of her champagne, savoring the taste and the feel of the bubbles on her tongue. Keith was staring at his sparkling water and tugging on Mac's jacket.

"How do they get those bubbles in there without a cork?" he asked with narrowed eyes.

"Good question. We'll look it up on the computer after the wedding."

"Cool! Maybe I can do my science project on it." He took a big sip of the water and coughed. "It doesn't taste like water."

Everyone laughed when he wrinkled his nose for effect.

"We're getting close to the time, Abbie," Mac said, checking his wristwatch. "Is there anything else we can do for you before the ceremony?"

"I just need to touch up my makeup," she said and decided to take her champagne with her into the bathroom. "Be right back."

"We'll be here."

She was dabbing on more face powder when there was a soft knock on the door. Opening it, she found her son, staring down at his shoes.

"Are you almost finished?" he asked.

Since she knew he had something on his mind, she didn't reach for her lipstick. She could do it after she discovered why he was blushing. Since she knew her son was too much of a teenager to talk to her comfortably while she got herself ready, she stepped out of the bathroom.

"What's on your mind?" she asked him.

He fished out an envelope and handed it to her. "Rhett gave this to me this morning and told me that you and I should open it together."

Wishing for her crystal letter opener, she carefully slit the seam with her fingers and drew out the folded paper. Rhett's handwriting was scrawled across the thick cream linen stock.

It is my intention on this day, January 23, to formally request to adopt Dustin Maven as my son.

She had to stop reading because her lips were trembling so much. Dustin took the top paper from her, started to read, and his eyes immediately filled with tears.

"Oh, man," her son said in a hoarse voice. "I knew he was going to do it, but it looks like—"

"He's sending the papers to the judge today," she finished. "Right after the wedding."

When he'd told her that he wanted to adopt Dustin, she'd never known anyone could ever make her feel so loved and supported at the same time. Mac had been Dustin's surrogate father for so long, but now Rhett wished to assume that privilege.

There was a card tucked inside the envelope, so she pulled it out.

To Abbie and Dustin,
I can't wait to make both of you mine today.
Love, Rhett

"Oh, good heavens," Abbie said after reading the card. That man got to her like no other.

Tears cascaded down her cheeks, and when she saw Dustin was crying as well, she hugged him to her.

"We're really going to be a family," her son said in a hoarse voice.

She stroked his hair, rocking him like she used to when he was little. "Yes, we really are."

And Rhett had known just how to make this day even more special than she could have ever imagined. He hadn't just made today about the two of them. He'd made it about *all* of them.

"He's the best guy in the world," Dustin said. "I'm so glad you're marrying him, Mom."

She kissed his head and allowed herself an unladylike sniff. "Me too."

She was more than ready for the ceremony to begin.

***

Rhett wasn't lounging with the rest of his buddies on the sofa in his hotel suite. No, he was pacing. And not because he was nervous. He wanted to be with Abbie and Dustin—his new family—*right now*. Having been raised a Southerner, he knew all about wedding traditions. Respected them even. Found some of them sweet. But when they got in the way of him seeing his bride-to-be and his future son, well, those customs grated on his nerves.

His mama, the wonderful Eugenia Lynn Blaylock, and his cousin, Charleston Belle Butler, had been henpecking him all day about maintaining wedding traditions. He'd finally coaxed them out of the suite with the promise of never-ending mint juleps in the Ponderosa Room. He loved those women, cross his heart he did, but they sure knew how to drive a man to drink on his own wedding day.

He wished his poker babes were hanging out with them. They would have sided with him—or at least he thought they would have. But since they were still trying to transition from their roles as his super hot poker babes to his dog walker and publicist, Jane and Elizabeth would be coming later with the rest of the guests. The plan was for them to blend into the background in normal clothes so no one would make the connection. Otherwise, the gig would be up before they'd even made the transition.

"Sit down before you wear the carpet out," Rye Crenshaw told him.

His buddies hadn't henpecked him about girly bridal traditions like his mama and cousin liked to do. No, they kept telling him to chill—like today was any other day—or they were lamenting the loss of his bachelorhood.

He gave his friend a hard look and continued pacing. "I can't stand all this waiting. Why did Abbie and I choose five o'clock for the ceremony?"

"Because it's closer to dinnertime," Rye responded, throwing a handful of salted cashews into his mouth.

"All he ever thinks about is his stomach," Clayton Chandler, Rye's deputy manager, said, kicking up his black boots onto the walnut coffee table.

"Good thing you and Abbie decided to go with that huge buffet," songwriter and legal genius John Parker McGuiness added from his perch on the sofa. "Otherwise Rye might have created a shortage with his appetite."

Rye's insatiable appetite for good food was an ongoing joke among them. Today Rhett would have hunted down a ham bone for his friend in exchange for help sneaking into Abbie's hotel suite for just one measly second. But no. Since his buddies were Southerners too—and sometimes gentlemen—they had blocked his plans, citing wedding customs and potential death.

The death part would most likely be at the hands of Rhett's future sister-in-law, Peggy McBride, who could pretty much shoot an apple from a pig's mouth at thirty paces. Not that he ever planned to challenge her. She was plenty scary enough without a weapon. Even if she was Mac's wife.

"Come on, bubba," Rye said, standing up and coming over to clap him on the back. "Have a bourbon with us before you end your days as a single man."

And there it was again. Another lamentation. "I'm *happy* to be ending my days as a single man," Rhett told them.

Rye and Clayton winced like he'd gone plum crazy and would end up sitting in a rocking chair on the front porch for the rest of his years alongside a broken washing machine. John Parker met his gaze with sympathy. If anyone had family man written all over him, it was John Parker.

"Y'all will change your tune once you find the right woman," he said. Not that they ever believed him.

"Can't ever see that happening," Rye drawled, shaking from head to toe in utter terror.

"Not a chance in hell," Clayton added through a tight-lipped grimace.

"Can't wait," John Parker chimed in with a grin. Rye and Clayton glared at him, and he held up his hands. "What? I'm serious. I can't wait to find my special lady and settle down."

Rye poured the round of Pappy Van Winkles and passed them around. "You're as hopeless as Rhett here is."

The door to the suite clicked open, and Mac Maven strolled in like he owned the place—which he did. "Since I knew you were stewing about how Abbie and Dustin would react to your note, I thought I'd come down to tell you they both cried."

Rhett's air passage felt like it narrowed to one of those small wedding tapers he and Abbie had chosen to light the ceremony. "She did? Dustin too?"

Mac slid his hands in his pockets. "Yes. Happy now?"

"I didn't mean it to make them cry." This was Abbie's wedding day, for heaven's sake. And Dustin was a teenager. What teenager liked to cry in front of his mama?

"Rhett, this was crying in the best way possible," Mac said. "I know I've said it before, but it means the world to me that you're adopting Dustin. Sending in the paperwork today was a wonderful idea."

"I'm the one who should thank you," Rhett said as his chest tightened. "Heck, I'm getting all choked up now. Mac, if you hadn't thought me good enough for your sister…"

"Enough of that talk," Mac said, pouring himself a bourbon. "Abbie thought you were good enough, and that's all that matters."

"She *finally* thought he was good enough," Rye added since everyone in the room knew she'd taken her time about it.

"Amen to that," Clayton added.

"Who's toasting?" Mac asked, extending his glass.

"I was going to," Rye said, "but I'm happy to cede the floor if you feel so moved."

"No, go ahead," Rhett's future brother-in-law answered.

Rye raised his bourbon. "To Rhett. One of the finest buddies a man could ever call friend. And to this new journey with Abbie. May the road ahead of you be easy and light."

Most of the guys threw back their drinks, but Mac only took a sip.

"Is this year not to your liking?" Rhett asked, narrowing his eyes at the bottle across the room.

"No, I had some champagne upstairs with the family," he said, waggling his brows. "Trying to take it easy since I have to walk the bride down the aisle."

Checking his watch, Rhett rolled his eyes. "Can't we start this whole shindig early?"

"No," his buddies all cried out in unison.

He sat down in one of the arm chairs perpendicular to the couch, crossed his ankle over his knee, and watched as the seconds passed until he could make Abbie and Dustin his.

***

When Mac returned from his foray to Rhett's lair, Abbie and Dustin had made a change to the ceremony. The idea had come to her after seeing her soon-to-be husband's note.

"Mac," she said softly, "Dustin and I have been talking, and if it's okay with you, he's going to walk me down the aisle like Keith did with Peggy. After what Rhett did…"

"I think that's a wonderful idea," he said agreeably, like she'd known he would.

Her makeup was perfect now, so she felt inclined to add, "And no more sentimentality. I can't keep retouching my makeup, or it will clump."

"You women are such a mystery when it comes to your beauty," he said, walking over to ruffle Dustin's hair.

"I'll make sure no one gets sentimental, Abbie," Peggy told her.

"It's too bad there's not a professional career in such a thing, my dear," Mac said with a soft smile. "You would be a millionaire in no time."

She only rolled her eyes.

"What's 'sentimental?'" Keith asked, bounding over to Dustin.

"Mushy," her son answered.

He giggled. "Yeah, my mom's not mushy."

Mac picked him up and threw him in the air, causing him to squeal. "But I am, so it all balances out. How about we play a game of blackjack to pass the time?"

"You're gambling on my wedding day?" Abbie asked, putting her hands on her hips.

He shrugged. "You *are* marrying a professional poker player. And we won't do it for money. Besides, Keith is getting really good at it."

"I am!" the little boy cried out. "Do you have a pack of cards in here, Dad?"

It warmed Abbie's heart to hear the little boy refer to her brother that way. Since Keith had a father, even though he wasn't present in his life, Mac hadn't been able to officially adopt him. But that didn't mean their bond was any less strong. She couldn't wait for Dustin to call Rhett Dad. And now she was tearing up again.

Peggy came over, and Abbie thought for a moment she was going to express concern over how easy Keith was becoming around gambling—something she was still learning to accept as a part of her life. "Your eyes look a bit shiny all of the sudden. Are you getting sentimental again?"

"Yes," she confessed as her brother and the boys commandeered a small table by the window for their blackjack game. It touched her that Peggy's concern wasn't for her son's ease around cards.

"Do what I do in that situation. I want you to think of the worst criminal on the planet, and then imagine yourself catching him and hauling him off to jail."

That's how her sister-in-law calmed her emotions? She was slightly terrified. "I...ah...don't know who the worst criminals are."

Peggy gave her a look of disapproval before shaking her head. "Okay, let's try something else. How about you tell me about your favorite flower? Everyone knows you're wild about them."

Now that she could do. She was in charge of all the flower arrangements at The Grand Mountain Hotel, and the flower bill for the wedding might have been as much as the liquor budget—not that she was about to publicly admit that. This was her day, and while she might not be a blushing bride, she was darn well going to be surrounded by beautiful flowers.

"The one I like best is a part of my bouquet," she told Peggy. Of course, her bouquet was in the cooler because she didn't want it to wilt before the ceremony. "It's called the Sweet Juliet rose, and it took David Austin fifteen years to create it."

Peggy's mouth parted. "Are you telling me some guy spent fifteen years of his life trying to make a rose?"

She made it sound like the man was addled. "Some

people chase criminals. Others create roses."

"Hmm..." Peggy said with a frown. "I'll have to take a closer look at your bouquet."

"You'll see the roses all over. I included them in the table arrangements along with lily of the valley." Sure, lily of the valley stems were ten dollars apiece, especially at this time of year, but their fragrance was too delicious to pass up the opportunity.

Even though Peggy looked like she'd just eaten a lemon, she said, "What other flowers do you like?"

If she hadn't already warmed up to her sister-in-law, that comment would have been enough to make her fall head over heels for her. She passed the time talking about sweet peas, peonies, dahlias, and orchids. By the time there was a discreet knock on the suite door, Peggy was looking over at the blackjack game with longing, which showed just how desperate she was.

Abbie went to answer the door. Her wedding planner stood there with an earpiece tucked discreetly into her brown curls.

"It's time," she said, extending Abbie's bouquet to her.

Everyone crossed to the door as she took the apricot-flushed roses and lifted them to her nose. The ribbon-wrapped stems were cold in her hands, but the flower's signature fragrance of fresh tea and lemon was pure decadence. Combined with the magical scent of lily of the valley, it created a perfume that was both sweet and exotic at the same time. The wedding and reception areas would be fragrant with it.

"So these are the flowers you were talking about?" Peggy asked.

She held out the bouquet so her sister-in-law could take a whiff if she wanted. Peggy screwed up her nose and cast an embarrassed glance at Mac, as if to say she was only doing it out of love for him. Then she leaned in.

She blinked rapidly before looking up to meet Abbie's eyes. "Those smell really good."

"I want to smell them," Keith piped in, bouncing up and down like a colored ball in a kid's air popper toy.

When he leaned in and took a deep inhale, she could only smile. He was the sweetest little boy on the planet, and she was so lucky to have him as her nephew.

"Wow, those smell really good, Aunt Abbie," he said. "Dustin. You should smell them too."

She knew her son wanted to roll his eyes—flowers were so not cool to teenage boys—but he did it because he adored Keith.

"They're okay," he said, his ears turning red.

The wedding planner fitted him with his boutonniere and then turned to Mac. She was Johnny on the spot, this one, which is why she'd hired her.

"Would you like to smell them too?" she asked her brother with a sly grin. "I don't want you to feel left out."

"I think the one on my lapel will do," he said, fingering the single rose fitted there. "Shall we?"

They walked down to the event space together, and her wedding planner touched her earpiece and mumbled something that sounded like, "The bride is here."

Mac kissed her on the cheek at the door. "I'm so happy for you and Rhett and Dustin, Abbie. Today marks a wonderful new chapter for all of you."

"Me too. Are you ready to take the rings down the aisle, Keith?"

He nodded eagerly and held out both hands so the wedding planner could hand him the pillow bearing the rings. Mac leaned down and whispered something in his ear, which made him smile, and then Keith went through the door.

Peggy and Mac slipped in behind him and disappeared.

"Wait," the wedding planner said suddenly, "isn't

your brother supposed to be taking you down the aisle?"

Dustin extended his arm to her and gave the woman a shy smile.

"We made a last-minute change," she said, feeling a little guilty she'd forgotten to tell the poor woman. "My son is going to do the honors."

Dustin puffed out his chest, looking much older than sixteen. "Rhett is going to get all mushy when he sees us together."

Yes, he would, but he would also understand the message. He'd made them all a family today by officially accepting her son as his own. Now, it only seemed fitting they both greet him together.

She heard the romantic strands of Mendelssohn's "Wedding March" begin and felt the wedding planner put a hand to her back to urge her through the door.

Everyone was standing and staring at her, but she pulled her gaze away from the crowd so she could find Rhett. He stood at the end of the white-carpeted aisle, his face radiating all the love and desire she'd come to expect from him. It took her a moment to take in what he was wearing. The blue-and-white seersucker suit fit him perfectly. Somehow his shirt, bow tie, and handkerchief were the same shade as the Sweet Juliet rose in his boutonniere. She'd expected a tuxedo, but when she thought about it, she hadn't asked him what he would be wearing. He looked every inch the Southern gentleman he always was in her presence—well, except behind closed doors, which was exactly how she liked him.

His eyes were misting over like Dustin had predicted. He broke tradition by taking a few steps toward her and Dustin when they stopped at the end of the aisle.

He grabbed Dustin in a hug. "Thanks for bringing your mama to me, son."

Her eyes filled with tears as their gazes connected

over Dustin's shoulder.

"You're mine now," he told Dustin, glancing back at her son, *their son* now. "Even if I'm not making official vows to you, I promise I'll be a good daddy to you. Always. I'll never let either of you down."

A tear crested down her cheek, and the ceremony hadn't even started. Dustin wiped tears from his eyes too as the two men she loved simply gazed at each other.

Then Dustin nodded. "And I'll be a good son, Dad. I promise you."

"I know you will be," Rhett said in a raspy voice. "Now take a seat beside your uncle so your mama and I can get hitched all proper-like."

Dustin grinned and then reached over to hug her. "I love you, Mom."

She inhaled his scent. Somehow even over the musky cologne Rhett had bought him for the wedding, she could still smell the little boy scent she'd always cherished about him. "I love you too, Dustin."

After their boy took his seat, Rhett held out his hand to Abbie. After giving her bouquet to the wedding planner, who stood discreetly off to the side, she clasped his hand in hers.

They turned to face the preacher, who was waiting patiently for them.

"Everyone, please be seated," he said to their guests.

She didn't remember much after the ceremony began. Her mind might as well have been filled with thick, fluffy clouds at sunrise streaked with pinks and blues. She heard the preacher speak and tell the story of how they met, but all she could seem to focus on was Rhett and how he was looking at her, how he was stroking the back of her hand with his thumb.

When Rhett said his vows to her, he cried through it, and so did she. When it came time for her to say her vows, her throat clammed up, and it took her a moment to recover her voice. Her profession to love him all the days of her life came out more like a whisper, but it didn't matter. The only one who truly needed to hear it was Rhett.

They exchanged rings, and by then, she and Rhett were both grinning like fools, their tears completely gone.

The preacher finished with a blessing, and it moved her to watch Rhett bow his head while still holding both her hands. She felt the blessing all the way to her soul. This was true love, the kind that came from some special design, something bigger than either of them. And she was grateful, so grateful, it had found her after all these years of being on her own.

"I now pronounce you husband and wife," the preacher said.

"This is my favorite part," Rhett said in a hushed voice, making her laugh.

"You may kiss the bride," the man said.

"You better believe it." Rhett pulled her close to his body and cupped her cheek. "My wife."

When he kissed her, she met his mouth with equal parts gentleness and benevolence. No one had told her their first kiss as husband and wife would feel different, but somehow it did. It was like receiving a beautiful quilt from your grandmother, knowing it wasn't just beautiful but would always keep you warm and remind you of all the love and support that comes with that magical unit called a family.

When they parted, she stared at him. He was her family now—her husband, the father of her son and any more children they would have together.

As they walked down the aisle, it felt like they were paving a new path together. And theirs was lined with the sweet fragrance of her favorite rose.

***

If there was one thing Rhett knew how to do, it was throw a party. Rhett surveyed the reception area. He would have been comfortable getting married in a bar strewn with white lights, but Abbie was a table-setting kind of girl, so they'd compromised. Whisky barrels covered with glass tops displayed the various food stations. He could see Rye, Clayton, and John Parker piling on the dry-rub ribs he'd begged to have on the menu. Abbie hadn't gone for his idea of including a whole spit pig, so they'd have to make do.

An old upside-down wooden soda box off in the corner held the cloth-covered jams and preserves his mama had brought from her lady friends in Natchez to give as gifts to the guests. She had insisted that she provide something, and since he knew his mama's bourbon-infused plum jam to be the best in five counties, he'd agreed after running the idea by Abbie. There was a simple chalkboard sign that said *Please Take A Jar As Our Thanks For Coming*. He'd already seen Rye take two.

Surrounded by his family and friends, he had the impulse to stand up on a table and make a toast to his new bride.

But he knew Abbie didn't much care for that kind of flamboyance. Plus, his mama would take him to the woodshed for acting like a deranged groom, even if the deranged part was simply because he was as happy as a lark. Usually she was the one who climbed up on a table, for what she called dancing, and he could only hope she might use a little restraint at his wedding. Which was highly unlikely, he knew.

He eyed his mama as she approached him. Eugenia Lynn Blaylock had never been a small woman. She joked that she'd popped out of her mama's womb with the God-given curves she'd proudly worn all her life. Her blue dress hugged her ample bosom, and she was already three sheets to the wind from all the mint juleps she and his cousin must have thrown back before the ceremony. She hugged him hard, her hands strong from all the sewing she'd done to provide for them when he was no more than a sprout.

"Son, you've done your mama proud, marrying that angel and agreeing to raise her son like your own. I can pass on to my maker now."

"Don't you dare talk about dying on my wedding day, Mama," he told her, hugging her back equally hard since she liked a good squeeze. "Abbie and I plan to give you more grandbabies to dote on besides Dustin."

She ambled back, her eyes sparkling. "All right then. I'll wait. Just not too long. Abbie, my dear. I just keep telling Rhett how lucky he was to find an angel like you. Honey child, I swear, you were the most beautiful bride I have ever seen. Who made that gown for you?"

Abbie found his hand. She was still a little daunted by his mama—like most people were at first. Eugenia was loud and feisty and flamboyant. He was a chip off the old block.

"I found it at a bridal boutique in Denver, Mrs. Butler."

"Honey child, how many times do I have to tell you to call me 'Mama?' I may have raised this rascal, but I look after my own, and you and Dustin are family now. Dustin, come on over here and give your Me-Maw a kiss."

If Abbie was daunted, Dustin was flat-out intimidated. Rhett's mama pinched the boy's cheeks every chance she got and fussed over him something fierce. Neither one of them had ever been fussed over by the likes of Eugenia Lynn Butler. It would take some getting used to.

Rye nudged Dustin forward, fighting a grin. "Get on over there to Mama, Dustin. She doesn't bite."

Even his buddies had taken to calling her Mama. Well, all of them except for Mac. Somehow his mama was charmed by how elegantly Mac Maven called her Mrs. Butler in that dignified way of his.

Dustin padded forward like he was facing the guillotine. Sure enough, Mama pinched his cheeks and then gave him a healthy slap on the back.

"You're going to grow up to be a fine man, Dustin," she told him. "I can always tell. The ship is still out on that one over there."

"Me?" Rye asked, pointing to himself as he swaggered over. "Come on, Mama, you know you like me the best."

Her laughter guffawed out as Rye swung her around like she didn't weigh almost two hundred pounds. She pinched his cheek too after he set her down, and he winked at Dustin as if to say, "She does that to everybody." Well, again, except for Mac. Nobody would ever pinch his cheeks.

"I'm so hungry I could eat a buttered monkey," Rye said, slapping Clayton on the back. "Let's go find some food."

"A buttered monkey?" Abbie asked, her eyes wide.

"It's just a saying, sugar," he told her, chortling. "I decided not to put that on the menu for today."

"Thank God." She took the white wine Mac handed her. "I need to wet my whistle to keep up with y'all."

He could feel a shit-eating grin spread across his face. She was working on her colloquialisms, and it was too sweet for words. "I need to find me a mint julep."

"Charleston, honey," his mama called out to his cousin, who stood talking with John Parker. "Could you go find me and Rhett two of those delicious mint juleps?"

"You got it, Aunt Eugenia," Charleston said, excusing herself.

"Rhett, I'll just go and make sure Rye doesn't swallow up all the food." John Parker glanced over his shoulder at their friend, who had made a beeline for the buffet immediately after setting Eugenia down, and then looked back at him. "You know how crazy that man can get at a buffet."

"One time Rye ate three whole ducks at this tiny Chinese restaurant we came across in Atlanta," Rhett told the group. "The poor owner asked him to leave. It was hilarious."

His mama guffawed, and Rhett caught sight of the Hale clan, looking over to see what the ruckus was about. He waved to Jill and Brian, Meredith and Tanner, and Arthur Hale, who was just about Rhett's favorite old man.

If he had thought there was a chance in hell that Arthur Hale would go for his mama—who was that man's junior by twenty years at least—he would have played matchmaker. But he just couldn't see the two of them coming together. It was a darn shame.

Charleston returned with his mint julep, and he loved seeing the fancy pewter cup piled high with crushed ice and topped with a swig of fresh mint and a black straw, the proper Kentucky-Derby way.

"I'd say y'all know how to throw a party," Charleston said, throwing her blond hair back over her shoulder. "Yours reminds me of a cross between *The Hart of Dixie* meets *Downton Abbey.*"

Rhett had heard of that British show, but he'd never watched it. Now, *The Hart of Dixie,* well, he might have watched re-reruns when he was on the road playing poker. He didn't do much carousing any more, but a man needed something to divert him.

"Why, thank you," Abbie said graciously.

He'd bet his front teeth she'd never watched *The Hart of Dixie.*

"I really like this little town, Rhett," his cousin said. "I can see why you've made it your home beyond the obvious."

He *had* made it home, which couldn't have

surprised him more. If you'd asked him years ago, he would have bet good money he would one day settle down in the South with a good Southern girl. But meeting Abbie had pretty much blown all those might-have-beens to bits. Thank God.

"You'll have to come visit us," Abbie said.

"Yes. Absolutely. You can stay anytime." Dustin blushed.

It was hard for a man not to blush if he wasn't related to Charleston. He'd even seen Rye react to her that way before. Her skin was all peaches and cream, her hair like cornsilk, and she had the most unusual shade of eyes—violet—which made her one of the most sought-after debutantes in Natchez. But she had a mind of her own and a mouth on her, so if you so much as tried to tell her what to do, God help you. Which was why she was nearing Southern spinsterhood at the age of thirty-three. Thank God she was a self-made business woman. She'd learned to sew from his mama since her own mother had taken ill and died way too young, and now she owned one of the finest fashion boutiques in Natchez. She designed clothes and sometimes still sewed them herself even though she employed a string of women to help, including his mama.

"That's awfully sweet of you, sugar," Charleston told Dustin with a smile. "Y'all will have to come to Natchez too. Rhett, you must bring them during Spring Pilgrimage sometime. Abbie, by the look of the wedding gown you chose—which is too lovely for words—you would go mad-hare crazy over the gowns."

Rhett cleared his throat. "Charleston, sugar, we might need to ease them in a little bit gentler than that." Pilgrimage was like walking back into another time with its antebellum reenactments, and if Abbie and Dustin thought his mama was something...well, she was in her element there.

"You're probably right," his cousin said. "I think I'll

go find me some of those wonderful ribs. Rhett, I heard you talked the chef from our favorite place in Memphis into giving the recipe to Mac's chef. You old dog, you."

He gave her a saucy wink as she headed off.

"I'll...ah...go help her," Dustin all but stuttered. "In case she gets lost."

"Charleston lost?" His mama barked out a laugh. "That will be the day. Even when that girl is off the beaten track, she's sure she's in the right place."

"Sounds like someone else I know," he said, and Mama nudged him in the ribs with an elbow.

"You need to grab your bride a plate, Rhett," she said. "She looks a bit peaked."

He turned to survey her. She did look a little drained. Likely from all the conversation with his family.

"How about we find us some food and sit over at the head table?" he asked. "We can talk to the rest of our guests after we eat." So far, they'd barely made their way inside the reception area.

"That sounds like a good idea," she said, resting her head against his shoulder.

"Where should we start first?" he asked her, surveying the buffet. He waved to Jane and Elizabeth, who waggled their fingers back at him. Damn, he loved those girls, but it was still weird to see them in normal clothes. Of course, Elizabeth's red dress had flair while Jane's tan one suited her more conservative nature when she wasn't in costume as a poker babe.

"I rather feel like some sea bass, asparagus, and garlic mashed potatoes," she told him.

Yeah, he couldn't see her sucking the head of a crayfish, and today wasn't the day to initiate her into that Southern staple. "That sounds like a great plan. Why don't you go rest your feet while I make you a plate?"

Her radiant smile was answer enough. "Well, my

feet do hurt a little. Why can't they make wedding shoes that don't pinch your toes?"

He leaned closer so only she could hear him. "I can't wait to lift your skirts up and give you a few pinches in other places."

"Rhett!" she cried out like she was embarrassed, but he knew it was only foreplay.

He said outrageous things. She protested for show. And they both enjoyed everything he'd promised to do to her once they were behind closed doors.

After bending down to kiss her cheek, he nudged her in the direction of the head table. "I'll just be a minute."

Of course, that turned out to be more difficult than he'd anticipated. Other guests wanted to offer their congratulations. He finally had to be as rude as a redneck drinking outside of church on a Sunday so he could get Abbie her plate of food. He prayed it wasn't cold.

"Sorry, sugar," he said when he finally reached her. "I got swarmed."

She fingered the edge of the plate after he set it in front of her. "It looks wonderful."

"Can I grab you anything else?" he asked.

"You don't have to wait on me, Rhett."

"It is my deepest honor, Mrs. Butler." He bowed at the waist.

"I like the sound of that," she said, spearing an asparagus. "Now, run and get your plate."

He was rounding the table when Rye, who was seated four chairs down, right next to Eugenia, stood. "Go sit with your bride. I can get you some food. What do you want?"

His relief was as powerful as drinking Alka-Seltzer for a hangover. "You know what I like."

"I think that's what your bride is supposed to say," Rye said with a dopey grin. "Take a load off, bubba. I'll be right back."

Someone brought him another mint julep after he took his seat. He'd lost his on his trek back to the table. When Rye brought him a plate, it was piled high with all his favorites. He dug into the ribs first. Took a bite of the maple cornbread and collard greens. Then he mowed down a dozen crayfish. And since Abbie hadn't agreed to his marvelous idea of providing wedding bibs for their guests, he stuffed his napkin in his collar so he wouldn't get BBQ sauce or crayfish drippings on his suit. When his mama started laughing like she'd uncovered a dirty little secret from Rye, who was seated on her right, he looked over and noticed the BBQ stain on the fabric above her bosom.

Since he wanted to keep peace in his marriage—even if it had only been legal for a couple hours—he did not point out that he'd been right about the bibs.

When he was as full as a prized hog, he leaned back in his chair and laid his arm across the top of Abbie's chair. Someone clinked a glass, and the crowd noise dissipated. Rye stood up.

"Thank y'all for giving me a moment of your attention. As one of Rhett's oldest friends, I drew the short straw today to give a toast to the bride and groom. Just kidding. I've known Rhett for a long time now, and I have to say, I don't think it will ever be long enough. He's one of the best guys you could ever meet. Generous. Loyal. A true friend. A man like that would be hard-pressed to find a woman who deserved him, but I can attest to y'all that Abbie is that and more. She is like the first sweet rose in spring. And she makes my friend happier than I have ever seen him, and for that she has my undying gratitude."

Crap. Rye was going to make him bawl like a baby if he kept at it. He dabbed his eyes with his napkin bib.

"Today they begin their life together, and I know it's going to last as long as their time on this earth. To Rhett and Abbie."

Everyone raised their glasses and echoed Rye's last words. After he drank, Rhett caressed the soft curls on Abbie's neck under her French twist. Her eyes were tearing just like his were.

Mac cleared his throat as he stood. "Rye couldn't have put it more elegantly, being a singer and songwriter and all, but I'd like to offer my own toast to the bride and groom. Abbie is everything Rye said and more. She's gracious and kind. And she has one of the most loving hearts you'll ever have the pleasure of encountering. I'm so fortunate to be her brother and to have shared so much of my adult life with her. And Rhett...well, Rhett came into my life when I needed a friend."

Mac Maven was going for a home run, Rhett thought as he knuckled more tears away.

"In the beginning, Rhett was as different from me as an apple is from an orange, but there was just something about him. He's one of the most fun people you'll ever meet and loyal beyond words, just like Rye said. It's been my privilege to be his friend, and now I have him as my brother. Welcome to the family, Rhett. May today mark your passage into one of the best parts of your life. And to Abbie. No other man could love you more or better, and nothing could make me happier than to see the two of you together. To Rhett and Abbie."

Abbie sniffed by his side and took a drink of her champagne. "I'm going to have to redo my makeup again after all this."

Then, from the corner of his eye, Rhett saw Dustin stand up to speak. Abbie was next to him, so she swiveled in her chair to stare up at him.

"No one but the wedding planner and Uncle Mac knew I was going to make a toast," the young man said, sweating under the light of the chandeliers.

Rhett's heart turned as soft as grits, and he reached

for Abbie's hand under the table.

"I've been lucky enough to know Rhett most of my life since he's one of Uncle Mac's oldest friends. All my life...I've wished he was my dad...and today he became that. Not only because he married my mom, but because he's started...the process to adopt me."

A soft sigh crested across the room as nearly every man and woman wiped away tears.

"Usually they say the bride and the groom are the luckiest people in the world on their wedding day, but...well, I'm the luckiest one because I have both of them for the rest of my life." He turned his head away from the crowd to look at them. "To my mom and dad."

Now Abbie started crying in earnest, and Rhett leaned across her to pull the boy down so all three of them could embrace.

"You're the best son a man could ever have, Dustin," he whispered through his own tears.

They took their moment, and Rhett heard soft music come on in the background as people resumed their conversations. When they finally broke apart, they simply looked at each other, love shining in their eyes.

"Okay," Dustin said finally. "That was intense."

"The intensest," Abbie said, trying to make a joke.

It made them all laugh. "We're the lucky ones, Dustin," Rhett said.

His son nodded. "Aren't you supposed to cut the cake or something?"

Yeah, they probably needed to do something constructive now, or they'd all be crying like babies in the corner for the rest of the night.

"How about it, Abbie?" Rhett asked her. "You ready for some cake?"

She rose from her chair. "Let me check my makeup."

"You look beautiful," he said, gazing at her loveliness.

"Thank you, but I don't think you could possibly see

a hair out of place right now." She excused herself.

She was right. That's why they call them rose-colored glasses, after all.

When she returned, they made the journey to the cake table. Abbie's apricot-filled Lady Baltimore with buttercream frosting was exactly the color of her favorite rose. He didn't like white cake with fruit in it, so he suffered through one bite to her two or three.

"Okay," she said with a sigh. "We can go cut your cake now."

Usually the bride and groom didn't cut the groom's cake, but he'd told her they would just have to start their own tradition. He was going to darn well make sure he had a piece of his own cake. Sometimes the groom never ended up getting a piece of cake in the melee of the reception, and the prospect horrified him. When he cut it, he knew he'd been right to insist. The chocolate was pure sin—just like he liked—and he grew light-headed after just two bites.

"This is delicious," he told her. "I might die on the spot."

She leaned in and pressed a frosting-coated finger to his lips. "Please don't. I have plans for you on our honeymoon."

He didn't suck her finger into his mouth like he wanted to, but by the slumberous look in her eyes, he knew she was thinking about how much he was resisting the urge.

"Later," he whispered. "Make sure the wedding planner packs us up a few pieces of cake to take to New Orleans."

"I already told her to snag some," she said with a wink.

"I like it when you're all organized and detail oriented," he whispered, pulling her flush against his body, not caring about the crowd.

The chiming of metal against glass rang out and

gained in volume, signaling that the crowd wanted a kiss. He was more than happy to oblige.

"Perfect timing," he said as he pressed her mouth to his.

She tasted of apricot and chocolate and was so intoxicating he nearly carried her off then and there. But his mama would slap the back of his head for his foolishness, and it would be embarrassing.

He finally was able to angle them over to Jane and Elizabeth. "Hey, girls," he said, kissing their cheeks one at a time.

"Abbie, you are the most beautiful bride ever," Elizabeth said. "Thank you again for letting us come today."

"Rhett considers you sisters," she replied. "You just had to come."

"And we're pretty normal looking, right?" Jane asked, gesturing to her outfit.

Rhett snorted. "I purposely didn't tell Mama, Charleston, Rye, or the other guys about your new roles yet. I wanted to make sure no one would recognize you." He would drop the bomb another time. Part of him was enjoying the secret, truth be told. And heaven knew his mama couldn't keep a secret, a quality the mint juleps would only intensify.

"You look lovely," Abbie said. "It's...nice...seeing you look like everyone else."

Rhett cleared his throat. "Ah, sugar. Isn't it time for our first dance soon?"

Elizabeth and Jane both met his gaze, trying to hold back smiles. They both knew Abbie was still warming to them, but no one needed a reminder of the over-the-top outfits they used to wear as his poker babes.

"I think it might be," she said. "Thanks for coming again."

Jane and Elizabeth hugged him and then headed off to their seats. Rhett signaled to the band to let them know they were ready. When they began to play the first strings of the song Abbie had chosen, he led her onto the dance floor. They swayed to "Night and Day" by Cole Porter, and she felt so good in his arms that he twirled her around like his mama had taught him to do when he was a sprout. As soon as he dipped her, she laughed with abandon, an unusual sound for her in public. But today wasn't just any day. She was happy. Happier than he'd ever seen her. When the song ended, he kissed her because he could.

"I have a surprise for you," he said and left her in the middle of the dance floor.

He signaled to Rye, who was standing at the edge of the room with his guitar in his hands. Keeping his gaze on his wife, Rhett took the microphone from the lead singer of the band. Abbie was already tearing up in anticipation.

"I wrote a song for my bride," he told the crowd. "My friend, Rye Crenshaw, is going to sing it for y'all."

When he walked back across the dance floor and took her in his arms, she squeezed him with all the love he was feeling inside.

***

Abbie had wondered if Rhett would write a song for their wedding. It was how he'd officially won her heart, after all—with Rye's help, he'd serenaded her on a cold winter night.

As she gazed into his eyes, she raised her hand to his jaw. "I love you. So much."

"And I love you."

Rye strummed the guitar and started to sing the words.

My angel wife,
Sent from above,

How did you find me?
How did you hear my call?

I've been calling to you,
Asking for you,
Praying for you.

And now, you're mine.
My love is strong.
You can trust it.
My heart is true.
You can count on it.

I will always be here.
You will always be mine.
And I...
Will always be yours.

When Rye finished singing, Abbie pressed her wet face against Rhett's suit and let herself go to pieces. How was it she'd become lucky enough to fall for a man with so much love inside, who bravely gave words to it for all to hear?

"You are simply the most amazing man I've ever met, Rhett Butler Blaylock," she finally composed herself enough to say.

His eyes were bright too, and he gently traced the tear tracks on her face. "I'll give you fair warning. I plan to write a song when we have our first child."

More tears swelled in her eyes and fell down her cheeks. Even though Dustin was a teenager, she and Rhett had talked about having more children together. They wanted to have the experience of raising children together.

"I can't wait to hear it," she said in a hoarse voice.

And as the band started playing the next song, she knew Rhett would be writing lots more songs about them, their children, and their life together.

She couldn't wait to hear every one.

***

Rhett had never imagined weddings could be this fun. Of course, now that Abbie's swanky band had turned the corner from more "appropriate" music to full-out country fun, the party was well underway.

The opening notes of "Cotton-Eye Joe" began to play, and Rhett turned to Abbie with a grin.

"Sugar, you've just got to dance to this one with me," he pleaded. "It's a classic."

She'd already turned down his offer to dance to "Thank God I'm A Country Boy" and "Chattahoochee," which Rye had played on the guitar with the band while singing.

She shook her head again, so he drilled his memory for a song she might actually grace with a dance. "What about 'Achy Breaky Heart?'"

Her delicate brow rose like she thought he was totally crazy. And he was. Crazy in love, that was.

"We can't dance to Frank Sinatra and Cole Porter all night." One song she might like finally popped into his mind. "How about 'Brown-Eyed Girl?'"

"Maybe," she said, picking up her freshly topped-off champagne. "Now go dance with your mama."

He was pulling his mama out of her chair moments later, and soon they were flying across the dance floor. Since she'd had more mint juleps at dinner, he had to keep a tight grip on her so she wouldn't crash into the couples looping around them on the dance floor. Rye was leading Charleston around in the mad dash that was "Cotton-Eye Joe," and before Rhett knew it, his mama had angled them over to the couple. All four of them did a little impromptu line dancing. *Touch, kick, triple step.*

Soon, Jill appeared next to him with Brian, who was laughing in loud bursts as his wife gave her best impression of a dancing Elly May from *The Beverly Hillbillies*. Even Dustin joined them, and Clayton didn't waste any time in showing him the steps. The kid didn't do too badly. There was hope for him yet.

Spying Mac at the edge of the crowd, Rhett danced his way over to his friend.

Mac took one look at him and said, "No way in hell."

He didn't dare ask Peggy, who fingered her waist like she was looking for her gun.

"I want to dance," Keith piped in.

Peggy didn't miss a beat. She simply responded, "Go find your Uncle Tanner."

The band switched to "The Devil Went Down to Georgia," and this time Charleston found him and pulled him away from his dance-averse friends. They started to twirl around the floor until his cousin tugged him over to one of the tables on the edge of the dance floor.

"Help me up," she ordered, stepping onto one of the chairs with her high heel. "Let's show these Yankees how we Southerners like to party."

Usually he would be the first one to volunteer to dance on the table with her—if it could hold their combined weight, that was—but he didn't think Abbie would approve.

"Maybe you should come on down, honey," he drawled as she planted her other foot on the chair. "We're not in Dixie."

"Rhett Butler Blaylock," she said, staring down at him with her hands on her hips. "Either clear this table, or I will break all the dishes."

She had that dangerous look in her eye that told her she wasn't messing. He started to gather up the glassware. The dinner plates had already been cleared, thank God. Hotel servers ran over to help him, likely at Mac's cue, and soon Charleston was dancing on the table. A crowd gathered, clapping to the peppy tune as she twitched her skirts and threw her head back and let out a bawdy laugh like a dancehall performer at a New Orleans cat-house.

Someone slapped him on the back, and he turned his head to see his mama dancing in place by his side.

"I used to be able to do that," she told him.

She'd retired? Thank God. He remembered her dancing at her cousin Patsy Lou's wedding. His mama had broken a table and bruised her ample behind. It had been a memorable night.

"She's continuing your tradition," he told her, clapping with the other guests now. Maybe that would cheer her up in her retirement.

"Everyone knows it's good luck," Mama told him. "It's a well-known fact that couples don't divorce if I've danced on a table at their wedding."

Looking over his shoulder at his bride's shocked expression, he said, "I'll be sure to tell Abbie that."

And with that, he made his way through the crowd to the band leader and requested another Frank Sinatra classic next to pacify his bride—and keep things from getting further out of hand. When the band transitioned into the new number, the crowd gave an audible groan. Rye graciously helped Charleston off the table, and the servers breathed a sigh of relief.

Rhett made his way back to Abbie.

"How about this song, sugar?" he asked.

She didn't say anything, only placed her hand on his proffered arm. The dance floor was as empty as a picnic spread after an ant attack.

"Your family is as crazy as you described them," she said softly, for only his ears.

"I warned you, sugar," he said, swaying with her to "All The Way."

"I like everyone's...spirit," she hastily explained. "I'm just...not someone who dances on tables."

He told her about his mama's belief that table

dancing at weddings somehow prevented divorce. And hastily added that she had retired.

"She should have gone on the road with her act," his bride said with a smile.

Now that was the smile that had made him fall in love with her. It was sweet and slightly embarrassed and filled with a restrained humor he found endearing.

"I can see the headlines now. 'Hire Mama Blaylock. Table Dancing Ensures Life-Long Marriage. Don't Miss Out On Her Wedding Reception Special.'"

They both laughed more easily.

"I guess it's a good thing she retired," he told her, leading her around the near-empty floor.

"Everyone hates my music," she said with a frown.

Rhett cast a glance at the only other couple who still shared the dance floor with them. "Arthur doesn't. He seems to be dancing pretty close to his date if you ask me."

Arthur and Joanie were the only people in the room who'd been alive when ol' Blue Eyes had recorded this classic.

"Oh, Rhett," she said with a heartfelt sigh. "When this song finishes, please tell the band leader I won't be an old fuddy duddy who denies the guests their fun."

He waggled his brows at her. "That's mighty kind of you, sugar. How about I teach you how to dance to 'Sweet Georgia Brown?'"

"How does one dance to *that?* Isn't it a song preferred by strippers?"

It was, but he wasn't going to tell her he knew that. Those days were behind him. "You dance to it with a lot of hip action." He pulled her close to his frame. "See what I mean."

She gave him a knowing glance, the fires in her eyes warming with each brush of his body against hers. "I do, yes. Thanks for pointing that out."

Swinging her around, he dipped her dramatically. "I

plan to point out a few other things when we finally find ourselves alone tonight."

"Funny," she said, running a single finger across his jaw. "I was thinking the same thing."

"Great minds," he said and gave her a soft kiss.

"Go talk to the band leader so we don't have a riot on our hands." She straightened her dress when he stood her back on her feet.

"Be right back," he said with a wink.

When the band began to play a jazzy, New Orleans-inspired "Sweet Georgia Brown," his mama let out a cry.

"Glory, Hallelujah, how I adore this song. I just have to dance to this one on a table. It *is* my son's wedding, after all."

Then, before he knew it, Charleston was helping his mama onto the table she'd vacated the dance before, making him wince in fright. He prayed it would hold her weight.

Rye, God bless him, hopped up on one of the chairs and grabbed his mama's hand to help keep her balanced. He didn't know if Rye would be strong enough to keep Mama from falling, but at least he could break her fall if she came tumbling down.

"It looks like she just came out of retirement for us," Abbie said, clapping in that elegant way of hers beside him. "Is your family always like this?"

"Yes," he replied with a shrug. "I *did* warn you."

"You did," she shouted over the crowd noise. "It's different though, seeing it in real life."

"Don't be surprised if we end up with a kid or two who ends up dancing on tables," he felt compelled to say. "As you can see, it runs in the family."

"So long as it doesn't involve a pole, I can handle that."

He snuggled her closer, ignoring the fact that his mama had just tossed one of her handkerchiefs into the crowd. It was about to get ugly. A shoe soon followed, which Clayton deftly caught.

Turning away from the spectacle seemed wise. Better not to look. "Why, Abbie Maven Blaylock, did you just make a joke?"

Touching a finger to her lips in a rather saucy and unexpected way, she said, "I think I did."

"Good," he said, pulling her close. "Make some more."

And she laughed long and loud as his mama danced on the table to ensure they would have a long and lasting marriage.

Not that he had any doubts about that.

Dear Reader,

This book has been so special to produce. First, you are the reason I wrote this short story collection of the weddings of our earliest Dare Valley couples. So many of you have written me to describe how much you love these characters and how they've become a part of your family. I hope you enjoyed their special days. I know I did, especially Rhett's mama and cousin dancing on the table. You can expect to see more of Rhett's mama and cousin in the future as well as the intriguing Asher Harrington, Tanner's best man. I have a feeling he's going to make some special heroine swoon with that sexy British accent of his.

Second, I was able to work with my incredible sister, Michelle Khamis, who was chosen as Best Wedding Planner of the Year. She's making brides' dreams come true far and wide at Dream Your Vision Event Planning. Come check out the vision boards she created for each couple's wedding under "Extras" on my website and our special Daring Brides Pinterest Board.

If you enjoyed this book, I would love for you to post a review since it helps more readers want to read my story. You can write one at any online retailer or on Goodreads. When you post one, kindly let me know at readavamiles@gmail.com so I can personally thank you.

To keep up with all my new releases, please sign up for my newsletter and connect with me on Facebook. I continue to post about lots of fun stuff, so come and join our Dare family party.

I hope you'll also check out my Dare Valley Meets Paris mini-series about billionaire inventor, Evan Michaels, and Dare Valley's own, Margie Lancaster, who's opening up Hot Cross Buns Bakery.

Thank you from the deepest part of my heart for expressing your love for Dare Valley in countless ways.

Lots of light and blessing,

Ava

Sign up for Ava's newsletter so you don't miss any news.

ABOUT THE AUTHOR

USA Today Bestselling Author Ava Miles burst onto the contemporary romance scene after receiving Nora Roberts' blessing for her use of Ms. Roberts' name in her debut novel, the #1 National Bestseller NORA ROBERTS LAND, which kicked off her small town series, Dare Valley. Ava's books have reached the #1 spot at Barnes & Noble and ranked in Amazon and iBooks' Top 10. Both NORA ROBERTS LAND and COUNTRY HEAVEN have been chosen as Best Books of the Year. Ava has also released a connected series called Dare River about the power of love and family. She's fast becoming a favorite author in light contemporary romance (Tome Tender) and is known for funny, sweet, emotional stories, sometimes with a touch of mystery and magic. Ava's background is as diverse as her characters. She's a former chef, worked as a long-time conflict expert rebuilding warzones, and now writes full-time from her own small town community. Ava is a big believer in living happily ever after and writes about her own journey on The Happiness Corner blog every Friday on her website.

If you'd like to connect with Ava Miles or hear more about her upcoming books, visit www.avamiles.com or find Ava on Facebook, Twitter, or Pinterest.

Made in the USA
Middletown, DE
27 October 2020